"I was wondering if you'd gotten lost."

A frown tugged at the corners of her lips. "Of course I didn't get lost in my own casino. I've had the run of this place since I was a kid. I know every nook and cranny."

A knowing smirk tugged at the edges of his mouth. "So you're avoiding me."

For some reason, Annalise's heart fluttered against her ribs. "No, I'm not."

A mischievous light twinkled through Luca's steel-gray eyes. "Admit it. You think about that kiss every time we're together." He shrugged, his wide shoulder rubbing against her arm and sending sparks of awareness through her body. "I know I do."

Hearing him say that should have made her feel better. But it didn't. It only made her want a repeat even more.

"I don't." Another lie. What was this man turning her into?

* * *

Blame It on Vegas by Kira Sinclair
is part of the Bad Billionaires series.

Dear Reader,

Enemies to lovers is one of my favorite tropes. There's something very satisfying about taking misconceptions and turning them on their head. It's human nature to jump to conclusions about the people we encounter every day. What they think, want and feel. However, these types of stories remind me that conclusions are often based on what we see on the surface, not necessarily what's real. And they rarely take into consideration that people are complex and situations are often complicated.

When I read enemies-to-lovers stories, I'm often reminded that kindness and love can win...if you let it. Annalise and Luca definitely have preconceived notions about each other. The joy is in watching them realize that not only are they wrong about each other, but they're wrong about what they believe they need and want in a partner as well.

I hope you enjoy reading Annalise and Luca's story! And I hope they inspire you to find the good in people, just as they inspired me while I was writing. I'd love to hear from you at www.kirasinclair.com, or come chat with me on Twitter, Twitter.com/kirasinclair. And don't forget to check out the other Bad Billionaires coming soon!

Best wishes,

Kira

KIRA SINCLAIR

BLAME IT ON VEGAS

HARLEQUIN

DESIRE

ISBN-13: 978-1-335-58131-0

Blame It on Vegas

Copyright © 2022 by Kira Bazzel

Recycling programs
for this product may
not exist in your area.

This is a work of fiction. Names, characters, places and incidents
are either the product of the author's imagination or are used fictitiously.
Any resemblance to actual persons, living or dead, businesses,
companies, events or locales is entirely coincidental.

For questions and comments about the quality of this book,
please contact us at CustomerService@Harlequin.com.

Harlequin Enterprises ULC
22 Adelaide St. West, 40th Floor
Toronto, Ontario M5H 4E3, Canada
www.Harlequin.com

Printed in U.S.A.

Kira Sinclair's first foray into writing romance was for a high school English assignment, and not even being forced to read the Scotland-set historical aloud to the class could dampen her enthusiasm...although it definitely made her blush. She sold her first book to Harlequin Blaze in 2007 and has enjoyed exploring relationships, falling in love and happily-ever-afters since. She lives in North Alabama with her two teenage daughters and their ever-entertaining bernedoodle puppy, Sadie. Kira loves to hear from readers at Kira@KiraSinclair.com.

Books by Kira Sinclair

Harlequin Desire

Bad Billionaires

The Rebel's Redemption
The Devil's Bargain
The Sinner's Secret
Secrets, Vegas Style
Blame It on Vegas

Visit her Author Profile page at Harlequin.com, or kirasinclair.com, for more titles.

You can also find Kira Sinclair on Facebook, along with other Harlequin Desire authors, at Facebook.com/harlequindesireauthors!

This book is dedicated to my faithful companions, Sadie and Charlie. You came into my life through different paths, but life wouldn't be the same without your goofy grins, slobbery tennis balls and energetic walks just when I need to clear my head.

One

"He's here."

Annalise Mercado took a deep breath. Luca Kilpatrick…just the man she didn't want to see.

Butterflies fluttered in her belly, although in the past two weeks she'd gotten pretty used to them. There was nothing worse than dread mixed with anticipation, which was what she'd been living with since Luca ambushed her at her brother's engagement party, and announced he was the savior her casino needed.

Bullshit. Annalise didn't need a savior. But more importantly, she sure as hell didn't need one guilty of cheating.

Cheaters and casinos didn't mix.

And Luca Kilpatrick was definitely guilty of cheating.

"Wait five minutes and then show him in."

He could cool his heels for a bit. Yes, her instructions might have been a blatant attempt at a power play. But Annalise didn't care. The man had dropped a bomb in her lap two weeks ago—surprising her with the information that he'd been hired to help her—and then simply walked away. No time for her response or protest.

The least he deserved was to be ignored for a few minutes.

Pulling out the tiny mirror she kept stashed in her desk, Annalise checked her makeup and smiled to make sure the spinach salad she'd had for lunch wasn't stuck in her teeth. She wanted to appear professional when she told the man to pound sand. The self-perusal had nothing to do with vanity.

Or the way her pulse fluttered when Luca came a little too close.

"No need to primp for me, princess." Luca's dry, amused voice washed over her. Apparently, she needed to teach her assistant how to tell time.

Heat pushed up her cheeks, but Annalise refused to let him fluster her.

Her gaze ripped down his body, cataloging everything as it went. The classical definition of tall, dark and handsome, the man was gorgeous and knew it. His features were classic and sharply aristocratic.

Beneath the expensive cut of his hand-tailored suit, his body was leanly muscled.

Luca Kilpatrick held himself like the entire world was his domain and he ruled everything around him with an iron fist. His steel-gray eyes missed nothing, which set Annalise's teeth on edge.

He was standing in the middle of *her* casino, dammit.

Rising, Annalise indicated the chair set strategically in front of her desk. A knowing smirk tugged at the edges of his mouth as he sat, almost as if he was the only party to an inside joke the rest of the world just wasn't smart enough to understand.

Rocking back into the chair, his lazy gaze traveled around the room. "Much nicer than the basement cell I was shown to the last time I darkened Magnifique's door."

The memory of that night, eight years ago, flashed through Annalise's mind. The sickening thud of fists hitting flesh. The way her stomach had flipped at the sight of blood covering Luca's much younger, but still defiant, face.

He'd gotten caught cheating at the tables, and back then, her father, quintessential old-school Vegas, had reacted to the situation much differently than she did now. That night had changed her opinion of her father, something she still struggled with.

She might not agree with her father on a lot of things, but he was the only parent she had. Her mother had been murdered by her stepfather when she was nine. While she and her brother watched.

Nope, she wasn't going there. Not right now.

Flashing her own tight smile, Annalise said, "If you'd listened to me, there would have been no reason for you to darken our door again. I'm not certain what Anderson Stone or my brother told you, but I don't need your help."

Anderson Stone was one of her brother Dominic's close friends and colleagues. He owned a premier and exclusive investigation agency in Savannah, Georgia. He was also the heir of a prominent American dynasty, and a billionaire in his own right. When she'd mentioned the cheating and theft happening at the Magnifique to her brother, he'd immediately contacted Stone for a recommendation and help.

Luca had shown up. Not exactly what she'd been looking for.

She'd already had a conversation with her brother about making decisions about her business that weren't his to make. The Magnifique might be part of his heritage, but she ran it and would decide who to hire.

Or not hire.

She'd been forced to schedule this meeting to undo the damage. And fire Luca. She really hated firing anyone, even him.

Part of her had hoped the meeting would be short and sweet, ending with Luca nodding his head in agreement, standing up and walking out the door.

Instead, Luca leaned back into the chair. The full force of his six-two, two-twenty, well-defined and eye-catching body settled in like he planned to stay awhile.

"Oh, you do."

Annalise resented how relaxed he looked. And how right he was. She needed help from *someone*, but it wouldn't be him. There was something about Luca Kilpatrick that set her on edge. She'd felt the first tingles of it before, but the full effect had slammed into her at her brother's engagement party.

"No, I don't."

He made a humming noise in the back of his throat.

"Look," she continued. "There's history here that Stone obviously didn't understand or he never would have hired you for this job."

Luca's wide mouth stretched into an easy grin. "He knew. Not only does he own an investigative firm, but I told him."

"You did?" Why would he have done that?

"I wanted him to understand that while he was calling in a favor, I had my own personal reasons for taking the job."

Annalise's eyes narrowed. "And what would those be?"

"I enjoy seeing the Magnifique falter."

"But you're willing to help us solve the problem?" That made absolutely no sense. The man just admitted he had no incentive to help her—other than owing a

friend who really had nothing to do with the problem.
And, yet, here he was, sitting in her office.

He shrugged. "I like puzzles and interesting situations that challenge me. It won't hurt my feelings any if it takes a while for this to get resolved either. The more money you lose, not just to whoever is stealing from you, but to me in payment, the better. I think the least the Magnifique owes me is a little cash after your father's harsh treatment. I had quite a few medical bills and walk with a permanent limp because of him."

Regret rushed through Annalise, before she squashed it down. She'd been too wrapped up in her own thoughts when he'd walked in to notice any limp. Maybe he was lying, trying to make her feel guilty. She would definitely be paying attention when he left.

"Well, you've just given me plenty of reasons to fire you before the job's even begun." Which was convenient.

"That would be nice, except you don't have that authority."

"I'm paying your salary."

"Sure, but Stone hired me, and my agreement with him was crystal clear. Only he can fire me."

Irritation bubbled up inside Annalise, filling her chest and heating her skin. What was with the men in her life thinking they could make decisions for her without consulting her? She hadn't agreed to that with Stone.

Apparently, she needed to have a conversation with Stone as well. But right now, she'd tackle the frustration sitting in front of her.

"That may be true—for now—but without my co-operation you won't be able to get the information you need to do your job."

Luca shrugged. "No problem. I'll just get paid for doing nothing. No skin off my nose." Leaning backward, he pushed the chair up onto its hind legs and rocked slowly back and forth.

He looked like he could stay right there for days and the gleeful expression in his stormy gray eyes suggested he'd enjoy it more if she fought him.

Annalise couldn't stop the growl of frustration that rolled through the back of her throat.

"Why don't you save us both some time and trouble. Give in and let me help."

God, the smirk on his face grated. "Because I don't trust you."

Luca shrugged. "Fair enough, I don't trust you either, so we're on common ground."

"And I don't understand how a card counter is going to be useful in helping me catch someone who's stealing money from my slot machines."

The affable expression dropped from his face as the two front legs of his chair hit the ground with a thud. His features, which had been gorgeous in a defined and easy way, suddenly took on a ruthless, sharp slant.

Gone was the glint in his eyes, replaced with something hard and intent.

"Shame on you. I see you didn't bother to do your research. What have you been doing for the last two weeks?"

Trying to stop the money bleeding from her casino.

"I've been a little preoccupied and honestly I wasn't interested enough in you to bother googling."

The corner of his mouth twisted up. "Princess, we both know that's a lie."

Goddamn him. Apparently, she hadn't been as successful at hiding her unwanted physical response to him as she'd hoped when they'd met the other night.

But she wasn't about to confirm his suspicions. *Fake it till you make it.*

Raising a single eyebrow, she tilted her head and silently called him an idiot.

Luca simply shook his head. "I own a software development company. I've written over a dozen successful programs, most of which you use every day and don't even know it. Along with my familiarity with gambling, probability and programming, I'm the perfect person to help you figure out who's stealing from you and why."

The same knowing grin he'd walked into her office with spread across his mouth again. "Like I said earlier, you need me."

Annalise sighed. Damn, if he was telling the truth, he might just be right.

* * *

Luca's right hip ached. He'd gotten used to the sensation over the last eight years and barely noticed it anymore. But it was obvious today. Being back inside the Magnifique had jogged several memories, none of which were particularly good.

Walking outside into the Las Vegas sunshine did feel good, though. With a smile on his face, Luca slipped a pair of dark sunglasses over his eyes and waited for the valet to return with his McLaren.

He'd certainly left the Magnifique under much different circumstances last time. Hell, now his cheek smarted, the phantom memory of skin scraping against asphalt joining the ache in his hip. He'd never forget the smack of the concrete or the way his entire body had ached from the beating he'd received at the hands of Mac Mercado.

Luca's sleek car pulled to the curb. The valet jumped out and passed him the keys, and Luca relished the joy of slipping down into the welcoming leather. This car was one of his favorite toys. He was fond of toys. He had money to burn and no one to care what he spent it on.

Just the way he liked it.

Pulling out into the heavy traffic, Luca headed away from the strip. While he appreciated the excitement and enticement of the casinos that drew people to the city, he preferred a little more isolation and space when he needed to think.

Which was why his estate was on the edge of the city.

Past the chaos, Luca let his mind wander to Annalise and her problem.

Annalise Mercado. She was sleek, confident, gorgeous. Arrogant and spoiled. Her chocolate-and-honey eyes had nearly punched straight through his gut when she'd looked up at him from behind her desk.

She was the type of woman who was all business, and he'd run into the sort more than he cared to remember. The way her soft, wide mouth had pulled into a tight line when she'd seen him... Not exactly a comfortable feeling, but one he was used to. Her entire face had drawn sharp, and unhappiness had flagged color into her olive complexion.

A part of him was gratified she wasn't thrilled to have him involved. But the rest of him thought it was a crying shame to use that mouth for anything other than kissing until she moaned out pleasure in the back of her throat.

The thought made his own mouth quirk up into a smile. Oh, the things he could do with her delectable body. She came off as cold and aloof, but something told him if the ice ever thawed...

The next few weeks were going to be fun.

His parting shot had been accurate. After the report Stone had provided him, it was clear Annalise was in over her head. She'd lost a lot of time and money trying to solve the problem on her own.

Which didn't surprise him. She struck him as the kind of woman who had trouble relinquishing control.

If only she knew control was an illusion.

The Magnifique was bleeding money. From the slots. But no one could figure out how or even for how long. The amounts being taken had steadily increased over the last nine months, so it was possible the theft had begun earlier, but no one had noticed.

The thief was getting greedy and eventually that would make him or her sloppy. In the meantime, Luca really couldn't resist a puzzle. Even if solving it helped the Magnifique.

Punching a button on his steering wheel, he told the car to connect him with Anderson Stone.

His friend didn't even bother with a greeting. "Tell me there was no blood."

An involuntary chuckle ripped through his lips. "No blood. But she clearly would have been happier if she could have left a few marks."

"Should I find someone else?"

He and Stone had had this conversation before. "No, I'll behave."

Depending on the definition of *behave*. He had every intention of doing the job he'd been hired to do. Eventually. As long as Annalise cooperated. He'd made a commitment to Stone, and that meant something to him. Stone Surveillance had tied their name to this job, so he wouldn't fail. However, that didn't mean he had to be in a rush…or keep his hands to himself.

His plan all along was to play a little cat and mouse with Mac Mercado's beautiful daughter. Given the family she was a part of, and her role as silent bystander for his beating, she deserved a little payback.

His best behavior was going to be very, very bad.

He hadn't been certain how he intended to play things until he'd walked into her office today. The woman was tempting, and if she'd been anyone else, he wouldn't have hesitated to go after her.

Seducing Annalise Mercado was going to be a pleasure.

She was fuming.

The asshole had breezed into her office, made a grand speech and halfway convinced her he was a second coming of the savior, and then disappeared again for three days.

It had taken a few phone calls, but she'd figured out where he lived and had to admit to being surprised when she'd learned he had an estate in Summerlin, one of the most expensive and elite areas in Vegas.

Sitting in her SUV, Annalise stared at the solid stone wall and huge metal gate that blocked his driveway. His estate was massive. Not just in the elite neighborhood, but the biggest mansion in the entire damn place.

Who the hell was this guy? And why had he agreed to help her?

Pulling in a tight draught of air, Annalise rolled down her window and punched the button on the small panel near the gate.

Nothing happened.

She waited for several minutes before punching it again.

Nothing.

It took six tries and her finally just sitting on the button before a grumpy voice answered, "What do you want?"

Narrowing her eyes, Annalise didn't bother responding. She simply pointed her finger to the gate in front of her and waited.

No way he couldn't see her.

A sigh echoed through the speaker, but a loud bang sounded and the gate slowly opened.

Annalise followed the long drive all the way to the front of the monstrosity of a house. She'd grown up in a mansion herself, so it wasn't the sheer size of the place that struck her. It was that it was *his*.

Her brain simply couldn't reconcile the memory of the young man, bloody and broken on her father's sidewalk eight years ago, with the handsome, charming, successful man he'd obviously become.

Stepping from her Range Rover, she looked up the wide front steps to the man waiting for her. One side of the huge double doors was opened. Luca stood there in low-slung jeans that were threadbare at the knees and practically molded to his hard body. The T-shirt he'd thrown on was slightly lopsided and just as tight. His hair was a rumpled, sexy mess. Like he'd just rolled out of bed. At three in the afternoon.

Maybe he wasn't as far from the cheater he'd once been.

But it was his eyes that had breath stalling in the back of her lungs. Sleepy, yet somehow intent. Like a lion lounging in the sun, perfectly relaxed but still with that predator's edge.

Tightening down on her response, Annalise forced herself to stare straight at him as she climbed the steps into his domain.

Never show fear or weakness. It was one of the first lessons her father had taught her. And while she might not see eye to eye with him on everything, that one she agreed with.

A frisson of unwanted excitement mixed with an edge of uneasiness rippled down her spine. Annalise didn't do excitement. Or uneasiness. She'd had enough upheaval in her life when she was younger and she went out of her way to avoid it now. She liked easy, steady. Safe.

And nothing about Luca Kilpatrick was safe.

She didn't bother with a greeting. The minute she stepped up even with him, she said, "You don't need my job or my money."

The corner of his lips tipped upward. "No."

"Why are you doing this?"

"Haven't we already had this conversation?"

"I don't trust your answers."

Luca shrugged; the shoulder leaning against the open jamb made a soft sound as it rubbed against wood. "That's not my problem."

No, but it was hers. She didn't trust him. However, after several more pointless days of staring at the reports, questioning their IT group and getting nowhere, she'd come to the difficult realization that she couldn't handle this situation alone.

She might not trust Luca, but she did trust Stone and Dominic. Her brother and his friend wouldn't send her someone who couldn't get the job done.

Raising an eyebrow, Annalise waited for Luca to move and invite her inside. When he didn't take the hint, she crossed her arms over her chest. "Are we going to stand here all day?"

"Fine by me, princess."

"Invite me inside so we can talk about my thief."

His pale gray eyes sparkled, and for the first time, Annalise realized bright blue flecks were sprinkled throughout them. Unexpected. Interesting.

No, she wouldn't let herself be pulled in.

A knowing grin tugged at Luca's lips. "I'm in the middle of something else right now."

"I don't care. I'm paying you. I'm here now."

He studied her for several moments before finally stepping back. The entryway behind him was huge, like everything else about his home. And, yet, he continued to crowd the opening, leaving her no choice but to brush against him as she slipped inside.

A zing of awareness raced down her arm where her shoulder touched the hard wall of his chest. Annalise fought the urge to shake out her limb, a reaction to the pins and needles response.

She sped up, practically speed walking down the hallway to put as much distance between them as possible.

"Last doorway to the right."

His smooth voice was way too close for comfort. But she followed his verbal directions into the back of the house, through an arched entryway and to a massive kitchen.

Modern with a touch of traditional, the space was huge. Gleaming professional appliances. An island big enough to serve a party of twenty down the center of it. A chef's dream.

Except it was far from spotless. Oh, it wasn't dirty, just used. A couple dishes sat in the huge farmhouse sink. Several small appliances were out on the counters. And there was a pan on the stove giving off the telltale scent of frying bacon.

Luca scooted past, once again brushing against her even though there was plenty of space around them.

He was doing it on purpose. Whether to intimidate or frustrate or short-circuit her brain, Annalise wasn't sure. The reason really didn't matter.

"Stop touching me."

Luca gave her another lazy shrug. "As you wish."

He walked over to a coffee maker, popped in a

pod and let water stream through to the waiting mug. He didn't bother asking how she liked her coffee, but poured in a healthy dollop of creamer and dropped a single cube of raw sugar into the mug before handing it to her.

How the hell had he known how she took her coffee?

Annalise was so surprised that she accepted the mug and had it cradled between her hands before it even registered. "It's three in the afternoon."

"So it is. We both know you live on coffee, so don't pretend it's too late for some. You drink coffee half the night. I'm pretty sure that's how you survive on so little sleep."

Annalise didn't bother taking a sip before setting the mug onto the granite countertop beside her. "You've been doing some investigating that has nothing to do with our thief."

Another one of those sharp smiles touched his lips. The man didn't smile for humor or joy. It was almost like he was privy to secrets no one else had figured out. Superiority in the guise of amusement. "I have. I make it a point to know who I'm working with."

"My coffee preferences."

"Oh, that was easy. You order the same thing from the coffee shop on the first floor of the casino multiple times a day. You also eat lunch at the same time and request dinner in your apartment on a set schedule."

Turning, Luca picked up his own mug and brought it to his lips. He took a healthy swallow, the long, tanned column of his throat working, before continuing, "You're predictable and boring, princess. All the fun and excitement of the casino at your fingertips and you never take advantage of any of it. Although, I will say, your employees are devoted and loyal. It's a bit sickening how protective and gushing they are."

"You've been talking to my staff?"

"What do you think I've been doing the last three days?"

Annalise threw her hands in the air. "I have no idea. You sailed into my office, made a pretty speech and then disappeared without a trace or a word."

"I was there. You'd have known if you'd been paying attention."

She'd have to get onto the security team. Although technically it wasn't their fault. Luca hadn't been on their watch list for years because he hadn't tried to step foot into their casino since that night so long ago. She'd be putting him back on the watch list now.

"I have a casino to run. I don't notice every person who walks in the front door."

"Which perhaps explains how someone is robbing you blind."

Annalise growled in the back of her throat. "My security team is top-notch."

"If you say so."

Her people weren't simply employees, they were family. She knew everything about each one of them, including what their hopes and dreams were. Annalise wanted loyalty out of her staff, and the best way to get that was to ensure they were cared for and appreciated.

When her entire world had exploded with upheaval and grief, the people at the Magnifique had been there to ground her. To take care of her and protect her. To give her a purpose. Taking care of them was just the first step in paying back that debt.

But something told her Luca wouldn't understand, so she didn't waste her breath trying to explain it to him.

"So, what have you learned in the last three days? Who the heck is stealing from me?"

With another lazy shrug, Luca said, "I have no idea."

Two

She was frustrated. It was kind of cute.

Annalise Mercado had a calm presence. He'd surreptitiously watched her and her team for the last several days. Security hadn't noticed him because he hadn't wanted them to. It might have been years since he'd done any card counting, but he still knew how to fly under the radar when he needed.

He absolutely enjoyed flustering her calm. Probably more than he should. The way her honey-brown eyes glowed and sparked…his own body reacted in a way that was both inconvenient and troublesome.

Being attracted to her would be helpful for his plan. Wanting her to the point that he'd turned away to flip the bacon not just because he didn't want to burn his breakfast, but because he wanted to hide the semihard evidence of his reaction to her, not so much.

"Three days and you have nothing?"

Luca shot her a pointed look. "How long have you been working this?"

"That's beside the point."

"Uh-huh." Pulling the bacon from the pan, Luca set it onto a waiting paper towel and reached for the bowl of eggs he'd already whisked together with sour cream, salt and pepper, and shredded cheese. Dumping the mixture into the pan, he enjoyed the quick sizzle as the scent of scrambled egg filled the space.

"Eggs and bacon?"

"I just woke up."

"That explains a lot." The tone in Annalise's voice left little to the imagination as far as her opinion of him went. Good thing he didn't particularly care.

Flashing her a smile full of teeth, he said, "The privileges of being filthy rich. I can sleep all day if I want to and eat breakfast at midnight."

Flexibility was definitely one of the advantages of being financially secure. Life hadn't always been that way. In fact, there were more nights than he liked to remember that he'd gone to bed hungry.

Annalise didn't need to know that, or that he'd been up until four this morning working on a particularly troublesome code issue in a new program he was designing.

With a sigh, Annalise walked over to the end of

the kitchen island, hoisted up the designer leather bag that hung off her shoulder and plopped it down in the middle of his cooking zone.

"Make yourself at home."

"Oh, I will. I brought the latest monthly reports so that we could look at them together. I've narrowed down the issue to the slot machines."

"So Stone and Dominic mentioned."

Her eyes hardened. "Stone and Dominic haven't spent the last five months poring over spreadsheet after spreadsheet of numbers trying to pinpoint the problem. I have. So perhaps you should get the details from me, the woman who spends twelve hours a day running the casino, rather than two men who rarely set foot inside the executive offices."

Oh, he'd clearly rubbed her the wrong way.

"Calm down, princess." Luca grasped the cutting board with a pile of waiting herbs and slid it farther down the granite. Purposely putting innuendo into his voice, Luca said, "You're obviously dying to show me yours, so feel free to lay it all out on the counter."

Annalise's teeth ground together, but she didn't respond to his jab. Instead, she reached inside her bag of tricks and pulled out a thin manila folder.

The front gave a hard snap as she opened it, using her palms to smooth it flat.

"Paper? What are we, in the Middle Ages? Can't you just email me the reports?"

"I did. Three days ago. And you ignored me. So, now we're going to go over them together."

Reaching into the cabinet above him, Luca pulled down two plates. He piled eggs and bacon onto both, reached into a drawer and added a fork before dropping one plate onto the counter beside the folder.

"I don't want any, thanks." The statement had been automatic, her voice even preoccupied.

"Tell me the last time you had something to eat and I'll let it go." Luca forked a pile of eggs into his mouth and chewed.

"I'm a big girl, I can feed myself."

"Then answer the question. It's a pretty simple one."

Annalise's eyebrows furrowed. She opened her mouth, but snapped it shut again before saying anything. Then reached for the plate, took a huge bite, chewed and swallowed. "Satisfied?"

"Hardly, but it's a start."

He knew for a fact that while she ordered food from the kitchens on a regular schedule, the plates often appeared back in the kitchen almost untouched. He didn't have to be in the same room with her to realize that she tended to get distracted and forget to actually eat.

Why it mattered to him, he had no idea.

Shifting toward him, Annalise dragged the file down the counter with her and began pointing to several rows of numbers.

"The algorithms in each machine are programmed for specific payouts. The sequence is randomized over a specific day, month, year, whatever the designation is for a machine. No one, not even the programmers or I, can predict when a game will pay out. But over time, there is a pattern that should emerge."

Even though he already knew everything she was saying, Luca let her talk. While she did, he studied her. And ate his breakfast, since he was starving and hadn't eaten anything himself since early yesterday.

"For instance, this machine—" her finger slid across a single line of numbers "—should have paid at a much slower rate than this indicates."

Annalise reached inside the bag and pulled out another pristine manila folder and opened it over the top of the other. "This is the report from last month. That machine paid out as expected. But this one," she said, pointing to a different line, "was almost double. The variations are inconsistent, but at least one machine—and up to as many as twelve—has been off for a little less than a year."

Luca hummed in the back of his throat. It felt like the right thing to do when she looked up at him expectantly.

"You're not paying any attention, are you?"

"Of course I am. Machines are paying out more than they should. There's no real pattern or consistency to it, except for that it's been going on for a while."

"That we know of."

Luca's eyebrows rose. He had a sneaking suspicion that the thefts had been going on longer, but maybe in small enough increments that it hadn't been noticed right away. "I assume you've pulled some of the machines off the floor to have the programming reviewed?"

"Multiple times. Each time, the machine is coded correctly."

"Not a coding error."

Annalise shook her head. "Not unless someone is managing to change the code with the machines on the floor and then change it back again. You're the expert, is that possible?"

Luca pondered her question. In theory, that might be doable, but it wasn't probable.

"Not likely, at least not without being noticed. But I'm going to want to look at a couple of the machines myself."

Annalise waved her hand. "No problem. Come by tomorrow. I'll have the head of our IT department get you access."

Oh, no, that wasn't going to work for him.

"No."

Annalise jerked her head up. "What do you mean, no?"

"No, I don't want to visit with your head of IT." Or, at least he didn't want to meet with the man alone. "We're working this case together, princess. Where I go, you go."

Her eyes widened for a second before she caught control of her facial expression again.

He'd surprised her. Good.

"Surely that's not necessary. I'm a very busy

woman, Luca. I have a casino to run and I've been ignoring it for weeks trying to solve this puzzle."

Luca reached over, snagged a piece of bacon from the pan and popped it into his mouth. "And you can continue to ignore it while we work through this together."

"I hired you to fix this and find the thief. If I have to shadow your every move why do I need you?"

"No, you hired me to *help* you fix this. *Help* is the operative word. I have my own responsibilities. I suppose we'll both have to figure out how to juggle everything. Besides, you need me because you're not getting anywhere on your own."

No doubt he could have easily handled this entire thing by himself, but what would be the fun in that? He wanted Annalise by his side while he did it. He enjoyed watching her squirm.

Shifting closer, Luca leaned down into her personal space. "We're going to be spending a lot of time together, Lise. Might as well get used to having me around."

Annalise stood behind the two men, simply listening to the conversation spinning between them. It was like they were speaking another language. One she definitely didn't know how to translate.

She was rather intelligent. She ran a multibillion dollar corporation and did it rather well. However, at the moment she felt ignorant and like an outsider.

It didn't sit well with her. At all. Especially since she had a pile of work waiting on her desk upstairs.

This was pointless.

Spinning on her heel, Annalise headed for the door. She was three paces away when Luca's voice stopped her.

"Where are you going?"

Her mouth pulled into a flat line, and she twisted sideways to glare at him. "Back upstairs. I figured since it's obvious I'm not necessary in this conversation, I'd return to the work that might actually be beneficial to the business I'm responsible for running."

Ice dripped from her words. She didn't get pissed off often, but when she did, she found it rather difficult to hide her response. If she'd spoken to any of her employees in that tone, they'd most likely have backed slowly away from her and left her alone until her temper cooled.

But Luca Kilpatrick was either oblivious, idiotic or spoiling for a fight, because instead of letting her go, he said, "Oh, get over yourself, princess. You're staying right where you are."

James, the head of IT, rocked back on his heels. His eyes went wide and his mouth dropped open. Great, five minutes after they left, the entire company would know how Luca spoke to her. Which meant she'd better have a good response to finish the story.

Narrowing her eyes, Annalise took a single, deep,

calming breath. She would not let this man get the better of her. Deliberately unclenching her fists, she strode across the room, closing the space between them.

When the toe of her black patent Louboutin heels hit the stark white rubber soles of his Converse, Annalise lifted up onto her toes. Without the heels she was several inches shorter than Luca, but with them she was only a couple away. She made a point to crowd into his personal space.

One thing she'd learned from her father—appearances were everything. She was not weak, and she would not back down.

"Do not call me 'princess' again, Mr. Kilpatrick. My name is Annalise. Ms. Mercado if you're feeling formal. You are my employee and as such are in no position to give me orders. Is that understood?"

A wicked light sparked deep inside those steel-gray eyes. The corners of his mouth twitched, whether with humor or with irritation, Annalise didn't know or care.

The low rumble of his voice melted over her as he murmured, "Yes, ma'am." How could his words sound like a capitulation even as something in the way he watched her suggested he wanted nothing more than to grab her, toss her over his shoulder and carry her off to indulge in sinful things together?

Taking another deep breath, this one laced with the spicy, tempting scent of his skin, Annalise took a measured step back. Somehow, even though he'd said the right thing, it still felt like a retreat. One the buzz in her blood didn't want her to make.

"Now, I have nothing of value to add to this conversation. I'm going back upstairs. Please come see me when you're finished." Turning to James, she said, "Thank you for your help."

James bobbed his head. "Anytime, Ms. Mercado."

Spinning away, Annalise headed for the door. She couldn't stop the brief sigh of relief that escaped as she rounded the corner in the hallway, out of sight. Her body buzzed and her blood hummed with a restless, uncomfortable energy.

Despite her last few encounters with Luca, she really didn't like confrontation. In fact, she typically avoided it. She didn't need a psych degree to understand that the inclination stemmed from her childhood and witnessing her mother's abuse and death at the hands of her stepfather.

She and Dominic both had been present the night her stepfather had gone too far. They'd been powerless to protect her from the abuse, and while her stepfather had never laid a hand on Annalise, she'd seen enough to be scared and carry those scars. And guilt.

She'd worked hard over the last twenty years to conquer her reactions and deal with the aftermath.

She ran a business and sometimes confrontation was unavoidable. Shaking out her hands, Annalise wiped sweaty palms against the sides of her pants.

Luca, though, was different somehow. Her reaction to him was…different.

Frustration still rode her. After so long, she thought she'd have conquered this response. When would the ripple effects of those experiences end? Reaching out, Annalise pressed the call button for the elevator. The doors dinged just as quick footsteps echoed behind her down the hall.

She should have known he'd given in too easily. Before the doors could slide shut, Luca slipped into the car beside her.

The irritation on her expression should have given him some satisfaction. But it didn't.

There was something else, deep in her eyes, that didn't fit. Something he was intimately familiar with from his own twisted childhood.

Fear.

Oh, it was muted. An echo. But it was there, and something he'd done or said had brought up the re-membered pain.

He'd seen the flash of it as she'd spun away. He'd heard the soft sigh of relief the minute she'd crossed out of the doorway.

And even though his brain told him to let it go, that it had absolutely nothing to do with him, here he was. Standing in the corner of the elevator, pre-tending he still couldn't see that shadow she desper-ately wanted to hide.

"I thought you wanted to speak with James." Her words were clipped. Annoyed. But he realized maybe the emotion was a smoke screen, directed at herself and not at him.

"I do and I will. I set up an appointment to speak to him later this afternoon."

"After insisting you needed to drag me down here now, you suddenly have something more important to do?" Her eyes flashed with fire, pushing that lingering shadow away.

Luca shrugged. "Apparently."

Annalise let out a huff. Bracing her arms against the railing around the car, she sagged into the shiny surface. "I honestly don't understand you. And I'm pretty sure, to save my sanity, I'm going to stop trying."

"Please." Luca let out a laughing huff that mirrored her own. "You couldn't stop trying if someone held a gun to your head."

"What's that supposed to mean?"

"Just that I know you."

"You don't."

He raised a single eyebrow, questioning her unwavering certainty. "I've been watching you for the last several days."

"And that's not creepy at all."

A smile tugged at the edge of his lips. She had a point. "I wasn't watching *you* specifically, you just happened to be everywhere. And that's my point. Your entire life is this hotel, Annalise. You spend almost every waking minute here. Hell, you sleep here too. Admit it, you're a workaholic with no life outside the walls of the Magnifique."

"That's not true." Her words burst out of her mouth and her body leaned forward, as if giving them even more weight.

"Saying it doesn't make it true."

"You wouldn't know hard work if it bit you in the ass."

"You don't know anything about me."

"You're a gambler. A cheat. I know enough. You're the kind of man who when given two choices will always take the easier path, no matter what."

"Easier, huh? Do you think counting cards is an easy skill to learn? Memorizing patterns, probabilities? I think you've allowed others to convince you about something without taking the time to actually learn about it on your own. I have a skill. Sure, it gives me an advantage over others, but can't people who excel at running or gymnastics or swimming say the same thing? They're born with a natural talent, but they work hard to cultivate that talent and hone it into a valuable skill. Casinos hate us because we take the odds, stacked in *your* favor, and even the playing field."

Annalise's mouth opened and closed.

Before the thought was even in his head, Luca found himself across the car. The heat of her body reached out to touch him. Just as his fingers itched to touch her. But didn't.

Both of his hands wrapped around the railing of

the car, on either side of her hips. It was the best way to keep them to himself.

He half expected her to hit him. To tell him to get out of her face. But she didn't. She also didn't shy away. Instead, she stood her ground, tipping her chin up and staring straight into him, bold and expectant.

"Go ahead," Luca said, "say what you want to say."

Her gaze raced across his face. He could practically see the wheels turning deep inside her brain. Finally, she opened her mouth, the tight pink tip of her tongue swiping quickly across her luscious lips.

"We've both made assumptions about each other, haven't we?"

"It's human nature."

"Maybe, but that doesn't mean it's right. Ultimately, it doesn't matter, does it?"

Luca leaned closer, crowding into her personal space even more. He wanted to feel her. To crush the soft curves of her body against the hard planes of his. "I don't know. I think maybe it does matter. I don't want to, but I actually like you, Annalise. You're bold, intelligent, unforgettable and sexy as hell."

She scoffed. "Unforgettable? I'm not sure that's a compliment. Trauma is unforgettable too."

Unable to stop himself any longer, Luca unwrapped one hand from the cold metal and reached for a strand of her hair. His fingers slid down the soft blond strand, settling gently against the curve of her throat. The warmth of her skin sizzled against his fingers. "Sure, you would focus on that and ignore the sexy-as-hell part."

"Sexy as hell is generic and easy. And you've purposely missed my point. We don't need to know each other. We just need to work together."

"What if I want to know you?"

"That's unfortunate for you."

"Take a chance, Annalise. Something tells me you don't do that often in your life."

Her breath sighed out between parted lips, but her eyes were sharp and guarded. "What I do or don't do is none of your concern. I won't be goaded into something I don't want simply to prove you wrong."

"But you do admit I have the ability to goad you into something. Interesting."

A groan vibrated through Annalise's chest. He heard it, but was close enough to feel the echo of it as well. "You could goad a saint into sinning."

"That's the best compliment I've ever received."

"It wasn't a compliment."

"Which makes it even better."

Annalise shook her head. "You're incorrigible. And dangerous."

"Look at you. Free with the compliments today."

The elevator dinged, announcing their arrival at the floor. Luca hadn't even noticed what button she'd pushed. He'd simply jumped inside the car to follow.

He was surprised when the doors opened onto the penthouse floor. Annalise used his distraction to scoot around and out into the hallway. Luca followed as she strode down the quiet corridor to the last of three doors at the far end.

She set her finger against a black pad embedded into the wall beside the door.

"Interesting. Cutting edge of technology. What's hiding behind this door, Annalise? Family secrets? A vault of priceless artifacts?"

The heavy door swung open, revealing the wide-open space of an apartment.

Sweeping her arm out, she indicated that he should enter. There was a silent edge of glee to her expression as she said, "My home."

Three

She shouldn't have let him inside her home. The minute he crossed her threshold, Annalise knew it was a tactical error.

Her apartment, while part of the hotel, had been her home for the past eight years. It was her own and she'd taken time and patience to make it exactly what she wanted. The space was open and airy. Windows everywhere she turned, except for the bedrooms to the far left of the space.

The view was breathtaking, especially at night. Lights, glamour and activity against the sprawling background of the desert.

She rarely let anyone inside. Hell, she'd dated men

who hadn't gotten past the front door. This place was her sanctuary. Where she decompressed and felt safe.

She expected it to bother her, seeing Luca walk through her living room, his fingertips trailing lightly across her things as he weighed and measured her safe space. For some reason, his opinion mattered, even though she didn't want it to. Which was why she pushed past him into the kitchen, grabbed a bottle of wine out of the fridge and poured two glasses. Smacking the stemless glass against his palm, she marched into the living room and dropped onto the welcoming cushions of her sofa.

Muscle memory had her kicking off her shoes and curling her feet up under her as she settled back to sip her wine.

Luca raised an eyebrow but didn't say anything as he took the chair across from her.

"I needed a minute," she finally said when he didn't fill the expectant silence.

"Clearly."

"Away from you."

"Oh, I gathered that."

God, he was a pain in the ass. "And, yet, here you are."

A smile played at the corners of his lips. "Here I am," he agreed, taking a sip of the wine.

The grimace on his face had an involuntary chuckle bursting through her lips. "Oh, it isn't that bad."

Gingerly placing the glass on the table beside him,

as if it might explode at any moment, he said, "I'm pretty sure that's the sweetest thing I've ever tasted. It's terrible."

Annalise shrugged. "Then don't drink it."

Luca sat back into the chair, rubbing his shoulders back and forth against the cushions as if rooting in to stay awhile. "Let me know when you're finished sulking so we can get down to business."

Seriously, she wanted to hurt him. By nature, she wasn't a violent person. In fact, she abhorred any hint of violence. But this man…he pushed her to the brink. And what blew her mind was, he wasn't trying to do it.

Sighing, Annalise let her body sag against the cushions. But her reaction to him wasn't his responsibility. It was hers. Luca was simply being who he was. And, sure, he pushed her buttons, but…why was that?

Oh, he was egotistical, high-handed and demanding. He definitely didn't play well with others. But at the end of the day, if he got the job done, wasn't that most important? She'd worked with difficult people before and managed to keep her cool.

Why was he different?

"Fine," she said. The sooner she got this over with, the sooner he'd leave her home. "What next?"

"I've flagged several of your employees and I'd like more information about them."

Annalise sat up. "What do you mean, flagged?"

"After reviewing your personnel files, I've identified those who have access to systems and security or are high up in the day-to-day activities and might have the ability to steal."

"No." She understood what he was suggesting but dismissed it out of hand.

"What do you mean, no?"

"This isn't one of our employees."

Luca dropped his head for a moment. Scooting forward in his chair, he clasped his hands between his open knees and leaned into the wide-open space between them. Suddenly it wasn't wide enough. The muscles in his arms strained against the cut of his shirt. Those strong, wide thighs bulged, drawing her attention down where it didn't need to be.

Oblivious to her distraction, he said, "I understand why you might not want to go there, but this is most likely an inside job."

His words were slow and measured, as if he was speaking to a child who needed time to grasp the concept he was trying to convey. Luckily, his tone killed her burgeoning awareness of him.

"Someone with knowledge and access," he continued. "It's ongoing and systemic, not the kind of one-time hit that typically comes from an outside source. At the very least, someone on the inside is providing information."

Annalise ground her teeth together. She understood what he was saying but didn't want to believe it. Her mind stonewalled the idea, refusing to let it take root. "These people are more than employees. They're family."

"They're not. You pay them money to provide a service to you. At the end of the day, it's a business transaction and nothing more. And if someone is offering more money, or they've found a way to make more, trust me, they're going to take it."

The expression that filled Luca's face pissed her off. A little disappointed and a lot condescending. Clearly, he thought she was naive. But as far as she was concerned, he was the one who didn't understand.

But the only way to convince him of that was to let him take the time to look and find nothing.

"You're wasting our time, but if that's what you want."

"Great. I've already had someone run background on those I've identified. Based on his search, he's narrowed down a list of about eleven people that I'd like more specifics on. I'll email you the list. Can you provide their full employment file? And because I know you probably know these people personally, I'd like to go over the list with you. Get your impression on whether you feel anyone might be a likely candidate."

"Fine." Reaching behind her, Annalise picked up the house phone that connected her to both the hotel switchboard and the main Magnifique offices. When her assistant answered, she rattled off several instructions. Hanging up, she followed that call with another down to catering. It was early evening and she was starving. She didn't bother asking Luca what he wanted to eat; she was irritated enough with him still not to care. She simply placed an order and dropped the phone back into the cradle.

If they were going to spend time together tonight, she was going to need something to sustain her. Something other than irritation and wine.

At some point, while she'd been on the phone, Luca sat back into his chair. His face rested against the ball of his fist as he studied her.

"That's rather convenient."

"What?"

"Having everyone at your beck and call."

"I don't."

His eyebrows rose. "Could have fooled me."

Annalise let out a huff. "As I recall, I had to track you down."

A wide grin split his handsome face. "So you did."

Five minutes later, her assistant entered carrying an armload of files. Setting them onto the coffee table in the middle of the room, she paused to ask if there was anything else Annalise needed before heading out for the day.

For some reason, Annalise fought the urge to explain why she'd requested the files. Ultimately, she didn't need to provide an explanation, but even the act of reviewing them made her feel like she was betraying the men and women who worked for her. Not just the ones they were scrutinizing, but all of them.

Alone with Luca and the files, her stomach twisted as she stared at the stack.

Dragging his chair closer, Luca said, "Let me make this easier on you," and snatched the top one off the stack. "Tell me about—" his eyes scanned the first page "—Christine Tillman."

Annalise wanted to say no again but knew it wouldn't make a difference. So, instead, she concentrated on cold, hard facts. That's what Luca needed to convince him that he was barking up the wrong tree. "Christine heads our accounts payable team. She's a single mother, although her kids are all grown or in college now." She didn't bother to add that the Magnifique had provided each of them with a yearly scholarship to assist with the cost of college. Or that Christine's oldest also worked for the casino. Hell, Luca probably already knew. "She's been with the company for about twelve years, I think."

"So, your father hired her before you began handling that aspect of the business?"

She didn't understand the purpose of the question but answered anyway. "No, I didn't hire her. Although, I don't believe Dad did either. We have an HR department that handles those decisions."

Luca nodded. "Were you aware that two years ago Ms. Tillman took out a second mortgage on her home to pay for her son's medical school? Or that she's up to her eyeballs in debt?"

"What?"

"I'm going to take that as a no."

"No. We offer scholarships to all children of Magnifique employees. I know for a fact both of her sons and her daughter applied and qualified. We provided them almost twenty thousand dollars a year. Each."

Luca's eyebrows winged up. "Apparently, that wasn't enough."

"That doesn't mean she's stealing from us."

"You're right. It doesn't. But the fact that she mysteriously began paying off some of those debts roughly eighteen months ago might."

Could he be right? She knew Christine had been dealing with aging and ailing parents, at the same time her kids were all entering college. Annalise had ensured Christine took advantage of all the programs they offered to help as much as possible.

But maybe that hadn't been enough?

The doubt creeping in made her stomach turn. Cold dread skated down her spine and the familiar anxiety she'd felt as a child crept across her skin, clammy and uneasy.

She hated feeling this way, and in this moment she hated Luca for being the source of the sensation. She'd worked hard to overcome the residual effects of what she'd experienced and seen, and in little more than an hour, he'd caused the physical reactions to resurface.

Annalise had known Christine for a very long time. The woman had been a part of their accounting department for years and was damn good at her job. She'd worked her way up and now supervised her own department. Did she have access to steal from the casino? Would she steal from Annalise?

No, Annalise wouldn't let Luca's words poison what she knew about her employees. People she'd worked with and spent a heck of a lot more time with than the man sitting in front of her had.

"Christine's parents both died about that time. Her mother had been diagnosed with Alzheimer's about five years ago and her father with cancer about three months after that. Coincidentally, they died within four months of each other. It was a very difficult time."

"But the inheritance was probably the source of the money, which is exactly what Joker discovered. But I wanted to get your opinion."

Annalise narrowed her eyes, staring at Luca. "Who's Joker?"

Without missing a beat, Luca said, "Our hacker."

"Excuse me?"

"You heard me."

"Isn't hacking illegal?"

Luca looked up from the stack of files in front of him, a dangerous grin stretching his gorgeous mouth. "Joker skirts the edge of legal, but he doesn't cross it. Often."

Tossing the file she was looking at onto the coffee table, Annalise didn't care when papers went skidding across the slick surface. "I can't be involved in anything illegal, Luca. That could jeopardize our license."

A single eyebrow quirked up. "Really? Your father didn't seem too concerned with breaking the law eight years ago when he beat the hell out of me while you watched."

How many times was he going to bring that up? Because each time he did Annalise's stomach flipped over and tied itself into a mass of knots. The memories weren't good.

"I couldn't control what my father did back then."

"You didn't do much of anything if I recall, except stand in the corner and watch."

Okay, she'd had enough of this. "You're right. I didn't do anything because I was young and scared. That night triggered memories that I'd rather not talk about and resulted in nightmares for weeks."

Luca's mouth twisted. "I'm so sorry you were emotionally scarred, princess," he said, glancing pointedly down at his right leg and silently reminding her of the limp he lived with.

Which made the knots in her belly tighten even more.

"I'm not discounting your pain, Luca. Or defending what happened. My father was wrong. Period. And we don't operate that way anymore. Haven't in a long time." Since she'd taken over the casino.

The aftermath of that night had prompted a long conversation with her father. One that had been years in the making as she finally opened up to him about what she and her brother had experienced the night their mother died. The violence she'd witnessed with

Luca had triggered memories of her mother's abuse and death. The absolute helplessness of that night and countless others. Things she'd never told her father about because the entire world—including the police—had believed her stepfather's story that her mother was drunk, out of control and recklessly fell down the stairs.

She hated that Luca had been the one to pay the price for the catharsis that had come out of his pain, but there wasn't anything she could do to change the past.

That night she'd realized that her father was human, and not always a nice man. It had been a revelation, one that hadn't been comfortable. She'd vowed to change the way the Magnifique operated and immediately put herself in counseling so that she could find a way past the trauma for her own well-being.

"What happened back then isn't what's important right now, anyway. You used a hacker to skirt legalities and investigate my employees without my knowledge. That's not okay, Luca."

Sitting back, he watched her for several moments. "You're right. I apologize."

Sincerity rang through his words, taking the wind right out of the sails of her irritation. She hadn't actually expected him to admit that he'd overstepped.

"Thank you." Dropping back onto the sofa, Annalise fought the residual, restless energy that buzzed beneath her skin. Somehow, she felt less than happy even though he'd admitted he was wrong.

"It's a violation of their privacy."

Luca shook his head. "Privacy is an illusion. Joker accessed readily available information in order to gather details on each of these employees. Sure, he has the ability to break into sites if he wants, but he doesn't need to. Most people don't think twice about putting their information out into the world and making it easy to find and track."

She heard the disappointment and irritation in his voice. "This really bothers you."

He shrugged. "I'm a programmer. I work in the IT world, but that doesn't mean I can't see the pitfalls that exist. For instance, your issue. Clearly, you have a vulnerability that someone has figured out how to exploit. We need to uncover that vulnerability and find out who also found it and how."

"And why."

Luca shook his head. "Why doesn't matter."

Annalise sighed. This was a fundamental issue she didn't think they'd ever agree on. At the end of the day, she needed to understand why someone would steal from the Magnifique, especially if Luca was right and someone from the inside was involved. She needed to know who among the people she counted as family could betray all they'd built and worked for.

"It matters to me."

Of course it mattered to Annalise because she let herself become emotionally involved in not just the business but with the people who worked for her. She'd built a family that only existed in her mind.

People weren't loyal. They looked out for themselves first, and maybe, if it didn't conflict with their own wants and needs, they might help someone else.

Luca had learned at an early age that you couldn't count on anyone but yourself. As a general rule, he didn't trust people. Or, rather, he trusted them as long as he understood what motivated them. Because then he could predict actions and reactions.

Saving time, heartache and headaches.

In some instances, Annalise was predictable and easy. She was a workaholic. Her entire life was the Magnifique and the employees who worked for her. She rarely spent any time outside the walls of the casino, and when she did, only a small handful of people were allowed close.

On that they were similar. Luca kept his inner circle tight.

But in other ways, Annalise was a complete mystery. The way her brain worked fascinated him.

The more time he spent with her, the more intrigued he was. Opening up another file, he began to question her on the other employees he and Joker had flagged as potential suspects. Without consulting any notes, she was able to give him a detailed background on each of them, down to their spouses' and children's names, ages, occupations and life goals.

These weren't her friends, not really. She didn't socialize outside of a work environment. She didn't confide in these people. But they clearly confided in her. Counted on her, and she relished the role of protector and provider.

An hour or so into reviewing the files, the dinner she'd ordered arrived. Spreading it out onto the coffee table, Luca sank onto the sofa beside her. They continued to work as they ate the perfectly prepared steaks, potatoes and salads catering had sent up. Annalise poured them both another glass of wine. His was dry and red this time and paired perfectly with the meat.

It was several hours later when they both sat back against the welcoming cushions of the sofa. Luca's back ached from leaning over files and a dull headache throbbed just behind his eyes. Arching, he stretched the muscles in an attempt to alleviate the ache and he let out an involuntary groan.

Beside him, Annalise stirred.

His gaze flicked over the stacked dishes they'd moved to the far corner and the scatter of papers across the table. He often worked late into the night. Or through the night, as he had the day Annalise had shown up at his place. But it wasn't often that he finished a long session like the one they'd just completed and felt energized instead of drained.

He'd enjoyed listening to Annalise. The way she stood up for people and defended those she thought needed her support. How she'd backed down when faced with clear evidence that maybe she didn't know someone as well as she'd thought.

There had been a give-and-take that he wasn't used to. And something about it was appealing.

His gaze traveled over to Annalise. No, something about *her* was appealing.

Her body was curled into the corner of the sofa. Clearly, she'd settled into a favorite spot. Her feet were tucked beneath her, tempting red-tipped toes peeking out. Her skin was flushed, and her honey eyes were clear.

His hands itched to haul her against him. He wanted to taste her raspberry-pink lips and know if they were as sweet as they looked.

Maybe it was the wine, although he'd only had two glasses. Or maybe it was just her. Because before he could talk himself out of it, he did just that.

She was light as a feather as he scooped his arms beneath her and lifted her up to straddle him.

Luca waited. For her to protest. Or slap him. Something. Instead, her head dipped and she was the one to initiate the kiss.

Her lips touched his and everything else disappeared. Sound, light, sensation and taste. All he could experience was her.

She tasted sweet, not just the wine that lingered on her tongue, but something distinctly her. His fingers wrapped in the long blond threads of her hair. His fists closed, grasping the silken texture and using his hold to maneuver her mouth to claim more.

Annalise opened for him, melting against him

even as her own hands grasped at him, hauling him up and into her.

A moan echoed between them. Luca wasn't sure if he'd made the sound or if she had.

Her hips ground against him, riding the hard ridge of his erection in a way that told him she unequivocally wanted him.

One minute she was magic and smoke in his arms, the next she was standing halfway across the room, her chest laboring on uneven breaths.

"No" was all she said.

Her eyes were wild and wanton. Her mouth wet and stained with the flush of passion.

But that single word meant more than the obvious signs that she'd enjoyed what they'd just shared.

With a nod, Luca pushed up from the sofa. He closed the space between them. Annalise held up her hands, warding him off. The way she twisted her head sideways, as if bracing for a blow, punched him straight in the gut.

"I'm not going to touch you, Annalise," he promised. "I'm going to apologize. I shouldn't have done that."

She stared out the window for several seconds, her mouth pulled into a tight line, before a heavy sigh pushed from her lungs.

"No, you gave me a choice." Her eyes were clear again as she finally looked at him. Disappointment punched through his gut as she continued, "But that can't happen again. I don't mix business with pleasure."

A ghost of a smile tugged at his lips. "Something tells me you don't mix pleasure with anything very often. Which is a crying shame, princess. You're sexy as hell and fire in my arms."

She just shook her head.

Leaning close, Luca whispered "Good night" into her ear. It took everything inside him to walk away.

Four

It had been two days since the kiss. Since then, she and Luca had spent hours together, poring over records and details, and discussing her business and employees. On one hand, the sessions with him left her feeling emotionally drained. Like she had to constantly defend herself, her business and the people who worked for her. On the other hand, she left each night keyed up from being in the same room with him.

The more time they spent together, the more she realized that she might have misjudged Luca Kilpatrick. He was intelligent, resourceful and purposeful. He wasn't interested in cutting corners or taking the easy route. If digging for the right answer meant spending hours analyzing reports, then that's what he'd do.

He was detail-oriented and difficult as hell. He didn't think twice about questioning any of her decisions or pointing a finger at anyone on her staff. Nothing and no one were sacred.

The more time they spent together, the harder it became to ignore the energy that buzzed just beneath her skin. Several times Annalise caught herself staring at Luca's mouth, fantasizing about kissing him again.

About doing a hell of a lot more with him.

But giving in to the urge wouldn't be smart.

She was walking the edge of frustration, not just because they were no closer to figuring out who was stealing from her, but because the longer they were together, the harder it was to remember *why* it wouldn't be smart to repeat their kiss.

Today, she'd needed a break. Some space to breathe. So, she was on the floor, making her rounds through the casino.

It really irritated her that now, when she watched her employees performing their jobs, Luca's suspicions tainted her eyes. She watched the dealers that much closer. Stopped, just out of sight, as an employee serviced one of the slot machines.

Annalise really didn't like the suspicion that colored her view now. Right after her mother's death, she'd dealt with something similar. Thanks to the circumstances, it had become difficult to trust the people around her. She'd worked hard over the years to learn how to place her faith in people again.

Luca had unwittingly taken that from her.

No, that wasn't true. She'd given him the power to influence her thoughts and emotions in a way she didn't like.

Purposely turning her back, Annalise strode through the casino. She was halfway across the floor when Luca appeared at her side.

"Here you are. I was wondering if you'd gotten lost."

A frown tugged at the corners of her lips. "Of course I didn't get lost in my own casino. I've had the run of this place since I was a kid. I know every nook and cranny."

A knowing smirk tugged at the edges of his mouth. "So you're avoiding me."

For some reason, Annalise's heart fluttered against her ribs. "No, I'm not." Even she knew the words came out too forceful to be believable.

Great. No way he'd let that go.

A mischievous light twinkled through his steel-gray eyes. "Admit it. You think about that kiss every time we're together." He shrugged, his wide shoulder rubbing against her arm and sending sparks of awareness through her body. "I know I do."

Hearing him say that should have made her feel better. But it didn't. It only made her want a repeat even more.

"I don't." Another lie. What was this man turning her into?

"Uh-huh." Skepticism dripped from the word.

Luca was clever. He'd put her in a position such that if she continued to deny it, it would look like she was protesting too much. And instinct told her that if she admitted she did want a repeat of that kiss, he'd have her pressed against the nearest solid surface with his lips tight against hers before she could blink.

This was a no-win conversation.

Luckily, her assistant striding across the floor toward them saved her from having to make a decision as to which outcome would be worse.

Maybe she let out a sigh of relief. She certainly felt it deep inside her chest. But before Amanda could reach them, Luca leaned close. The warmth of his breath brushed against her skin as he whispered, "This conversation isn't over."

Oh, yes it was. Conversation required two people and she wasn't interested in participating. But she wasn't about to say that to him right now.

"Ms. Mercado, I'm sorry to bother you while you're on the floor, but we have a situation upstairs that I know you'd want to be aware of."

Glancing over at Luca, she offered him an apologetic smile that she really didn't feel. "Excuse me," she murmured, and left to follow her assistant.

Unfortunately, Luca didn't take the hint and kept step with her as they crossed to the door leading into the back of the house and up the elevator to the executive floor.

Employee offices were scattered throughout the casino. But up here, most of the departments were for the executive staffs, human resources, accounting. Amanda led her through to the head of the catering suite. The group handled all the restaurants, cafés and bars within the casino, room service, large catered events and the waitstaff. And sitting just inside the door to the group of offices was a young woman with dried tear tracks down her face.

Annalise swept into the offices, crouched down before Carmen, the woman, and grasped her hands. "What's wrong? What happened?"

Carmen's big brown eyes went shimmery with new tears as several slipped over her lower lashes. She shook her head, her throat working even as her lips trembled.

Behind her, Amanda reached for a tissue and offered it to the other woman. "Carmen just received word that her father and brother were involved in a car accident. Her father was med-flighted and her brother rushed by ambulance to the hospital."

Without looking over her shoulder, Annalise said, "Let's get her a ride. Which hospital were they taken to?"

"They're in Chicago."

Squeezing Carmen's hands, Annalise asked, "Is there anyone here we can call to come get you?"

Carmen finally found her voice. It wobbled as she spoke. "My roommate is already on her way."

"Good. That's good. Amanda is going to book you on the first flight to Chicago."

Carmen shook her head, the avalanche of tears cresting over her lashes again. "I can't afford a plane ticket."

Annalise's heart ached for the young woman. The fear and uncertainty that must be eating at her. The knowledge that she didn't have the resources to get back home and be with her family when they needed her most. Nope, that wasn't going to happen on her watch.

"You misunderstand. I'm paying for your plane ticket. If your roommate can go with you, I'm happy to book her a ticket as well. You need to be with your family right now, Carmen. And I'll do whatever I can to make that happen."

Carmen's face crumpled. At first, Annalise thought it was with grief, but as Carmen flung her arms around Annalise's shoulders, she realized it was in gratitude.

"Thank you," she whispered. "Thank you."

Annalise patted her hands across Carmen's back, offering what little comfort she could. "Take as much time as you need. Please let the head of catering know how your father and brother are doing and if there's anything else we can do to help."

Annalise held the young woman. She let her cry out her fear and grief, process the unexpected trauma. Ten minutes later, her roommate was escorted up to the suite. Amanda spoke softly to her, no doubt trying to get the details she'd need in order to book flights.

Annalise gently extracted herself, passing Carmen over to Amanda's capable hands. She knew her assistant would cover everything just as she would want. Walking back into the hallway, Annalise realized Luca was still standing there, leaning against the wall, simply waiting.

She'd forgotten he was there.

One ankle crossed over the other, hands shoved deep into the pockets of his slacks, his stormy eyes watched her. Studied her in a way that made her feel...stalked. In that moment, she wanted to turn around and rush back into the room. Embrace the safety of others so she wouldn't have to confront the man standing here, waiting.

But she wasn't a coward. And she wouldn't let herself be intimidated. Especially by Luca.

"I'm sorry. You didn't need to wait. You could have gone back up to my office."

"And miss the show?"

Annalise's eyebrows beetled. "Show? You think a young woman's fear for her family, grief at being so far away and helplessness because she didn't think she was going to be able to get to them is entertainment?"

What the hell was wrong with him?

"No. I wasn't referring to her. What she's dealing with is tragic. It sucks. But it's life, isn't it? Bad things happen to good people every day."

The way he said the words, matter-of-fact and bone-deep, told her he'd experienced his own version of tragedy more than once. Something inside her ached at that thought.

But not enough to let what he'd said pass. "Maybe so, but does that mean those people don't deserve compassion?"

"Of course not. They do."

Annalise clenched her own fists into tight balls. "I don't understand what you mean, then."

"I was talking about you. Annalise, the savior."

Okay, now he was really pissing her off. "Helping someone who needs it doesn't make me a savior." It made her compassionate and understanding, both good qualities as far as she was concerned.

Luca's skeptical expression returned. "Most bosses would have ensured she got home. Calling her room-mate to come get her is about as far as most employers would have gone. You went above and beyond, Annalise."

"God forbid. I have the ability to solve a major problem in that woman's life with little to no impact on my own existence. To take some of the pressure off in a moment where she's dealing with so much. I'd be a bitch if I didn't help."

"No, you'd be normal."

Annalise threw up her hands, frustrated beyond belief. "Then I don't want to be normal."

The edges of Luca's lips fluttered, although she wasn't sure if it was in preparation for a smile or a frown. "I'm starting to realize that's very true."

Luca didn't want to actually like Annalise.

He wanted to remember the young woman who'd stood in the corner of the room, silent, as she watched her father order two men to beat him senseless. He wanted to hate her. To let her carry the blame for the physical damage that had been done to him.

But he couldn't, dammit.

She wasn't ruthless and uncaring like her father. Clearly.

It wasn't simply the way she'd helped Carmen, although that was part of it. It was the fact that she hadn't even thought twice about it before offering the help. There was no calculation behind the action, which in his world was like finding a unicorn. No one did anything without an ulterior motive.

Except Annalise.

Something that had been so simple for her to do had hugely impacted the other woman's life. And even as she'd done it, Annalise didn't truly understand.

He did. Because there was a time in his life that he'd been in a situation similar to Carmen's. Destitute, emotionally devastated, without anyone to care for or comfort him.

From the time he was seven, the only person he could count on was himself. Hell, even before then. He'd always been alone. No family, no one to claim him or care.

He envied Carmen. And Annalise, for that matter.

She actually cared for the people around her. Really and truly cared. Which he knew was rare.

No one had ever cared about him. He'd never been a part of a family, not a real one and not the kind that she'd built at the Magnifique.

Somewhere deep inside, a kernel of want popped

open inside him. It wasn't simply physical, because he'd physically wanted her from the moment he'd laid eyes on her. This was more.

He'd convinced himself, a long time ago, that he didn't want or need the kind of existence Annalise thrived on. Being part of a larger whole. Relying on others. Depending on them for things, which would only lead to disappointment. Or, more, owing them responsibility and loyalty. Annalise wasn't just a part of the larger whole but she was the calm eye in the center of the storm.

Luca laughed at himself. That conviction had been self-preservation at its finest. Because by the time he hit his early teens, Luca was keenly aware that no dramatic after-school special was going to play out in his life. No long-lost relative would claim him. No perfect and quirky couple would decide to adopt him so he could fill the hole in their family.

Now, at thirty, he realized that he did actually want what Annalise had. Connection. People to combat the loneliness. Someone to call him on his bullshit and tell him when he was being an ass. Someone to make him laugh and smile.

The kicker was, he still wasn't going to get it. Because that's not how life worked.

Or his life.

Instead, maybe he'd simply take what he could get and enjoy being on the periphery of the comfort and support while he had the chance.

No question, he definitely wanted her. And that

need wasn't simply driven by a physical desire for her, although the drive to touch and taste every inch of her skin overwhelmed him. Like all the other puzzles or problems he spent his life solving, he needed to dissect her and understand.

What was it about Annalise that drew people to her? That convinced others to trust her and confide in her?

He honestly didn't understand, but he wanted to.

She strode beside him as they both walked through the casino. It was late by most standards, but early in the casino world. Flipping his wrist over, Luca registered that it was almost midnight, not that he could tell by looking around him. Neon lights, loud noises and people filled the floor.

Luca's footsteps slowed, not necessarily because he cared what was happening around him, but because he wasn't ready to let her go. It was a delaying tactic, and he knew it.

Turning away from the path to the exit, Luca wandered through a row of slot machines. Annalise took a handful of steps in the opposite direction before she realized he'd taken a detour and turned to follow.

Until this job at the Magnifique, it had been a long time since he'd been on the floor of a casino. For the first time, he realized that the sounds he was hearing were…wrong. Oh, the machines whirred. Bells and whistles sounded. And the background noise of rollers speeding up and dropping into place accompanied it all.

But the sounds were generic and too perfect.

The metallic clank of coins dropping into the slots was digitized, not real. None of the machines actually had mechanisms that spun. Everything was digital, simulated on a screen.

Logically, he'd recognized that fact. Hell, he developed IT programs for a living. He knew just how powerful code could be. But he hadn't fully put two and two together.

As he watched the men and women sitting at the machines, he realized they no longer carried little buckets to collect their coins. Every machine had a slot and the ones that were occupied had a card pushed into it.

"What are the cards they're using?" He didn't bother turning around to look at her, he knew Annalise was there. He could feel her in the buzz running through his blood.

"Those are player cards. All the slot machines take them. The tables still use cash and chips, although we have some digital machines for some of those games as well."

"They function like a debit card? Money in and money out?"

"Yes, among other things."

"What other things?" His words rushed out, his mind spinning quickly as he cataloged the possibilities and impact of what she was saying.

Annalise's eyebrows furrowed, his question clearly confusing her. But she answered anyway. "Just like any other tracking mechanism, we use the cards to gather data. We can identify our regular players and reward them for their loyalty. We track winnings and losses and provide incentives for both groups of players."

Luca laughed. "Meaning Aunt Millie just won three thousand on a machine, you're going to magically offer her an upgraded and extended stay so she hopefully loses it back to the house."

Annalise frowned. "You make it sound cold and callous. We don't target winners specifically. We gather data trends. What machines are being overlooked? Which ones are preferred? What marketing tools are effective?"

Luca nodded, understanding exactly where she was going. The cards provided a way to more efficiently run the business. "Which machines are paying out more than their algorithms indicate they should."

"Exactly."

"But you do use the cards to reward your big players?"

Annalise's gaze made a quick tour of the floor before returning to him. "Absolutely. They operate on a points system. Players earn points for specific things and receive rewards at various levels."

"Even your whales?" High rollers were commonly referred to as "whales." They often brought big money to the tables, but also dropped plenty of coin on suites, food, beverages and amenities. They were often given preferential treatment.

"Of course. They don't always like keeping up with the loyalty cards, but for our higher stakes tables our staff ensure they receive credit for their play."

Luca glanced around him. He wasn't as concerned with the players who preferred table games like poker and blackjack. Annalise was most likely losing some money at those tables through card counting or cheating, but that wasn't the problem she'd hired him to solve. His concern was directly tied to the slot machines.

Spinning around to look at her, Luca realized she was closer than he'd expected. His hand brushed against the tight line of her upper thigh. Instinctively, he reached for her, his palm wrapping around the flared curve of her waist as he pulled her close.

Her breath caught in her throat. Luca heard the quick catch and felt the stuttered rise and fall as her breasts rubbed against his chest.

Annalise looked up at him, those honey eyes wide and stunned. But that startled expression quickly melted away, turning into a blazing heat that ripped through his gut.

Placing her own hands over his, Annalise jerked his arms out and held them wide as she took a single step backward.

Her control both impressed and frustrated him.

But at the moment, they weren't exactly somewhere he wanted to press her on that reaction. Even the boss was under the eye of surveillance. Maybe especially the boss.

"I need a list of your highest grossing loyalty point earners exclusively from the slot machines."

The corner of Annalise's eyes crinkled as she narrowed her gaze in thought. "You're thinking we can track the increase in play over the last several months through the loyalty points and try to match the trend we've identified at the machines."

"Exactly. It won't be perfect, but maybe we can narrow down the list enough to get a good idea."

Her head tipped sideways. "Okay, so maybe we identify a list of suspects... That doesn't explain how they're stealing the money."

Luca had to admit, she had a point. "No, but it's a place to start."

Five

This was becoming a habit. One Annalise didn't like. Not twelve hours after she'd provided him the list from her analytics team and Luca had already found a way to use it to piss her off.

Storming into the office Luca had taken over, she slammed the door into the wall behind her. If she'd been a little less angry, she would have stopped long enough to be concerned about possible drywall damage. But at the moment, she couldn't think of anything except how angry she was.

She'd just spent twenty minutes talking down a high roller from the tirade sparked by a phone call from Luca. Running this business was difficult enough without Luca doing his best to alienate her best clients.

"What the hell do you think you're doing?"

Luca glanced up at her. His gaze ripped down her body and back up again, before returning to the computer screen in front of him.

"I'm trying to figure out how the programming for your little loyalty cards works."

"Funny, because according to the phone call I just received, it sounded to me like you've been harassing Magnifique customers."

The corners of his lips tugged up into a quick grin, but the man was smart enough to erase it before returning his focus to her.

"I'm sure I don't know what you're talking about."

"Bullshit. You know exactly what I'm talking about. I didn't provide you with the information on our customers so you could harass them."

"I hardly think the conversation rose to harassment."

"Well, Mr. Harding's opinion clearly differs from yours. He felt attacked. I just spent the last twenty minutes calming him down and convincing him that the Magnifique wasn't using the player card in order to keep tabs on his habits."

"But you are."

"Yes, we are. And Mr. Harding is smart enough to know that. But there's a difference between knowing it's probably happening and still choosing to use the card because you like the benefits, and having the knowledge shoved down your throat while someone minutely questions you about your spending habits at the casino over the last year."

Luca shook his head. "He's an asshole."

"No, from where I'm sitting, you're the asshole. Luca, you can't treat our customers that way. If you do, we won't have customers for very long. Is that what you want? Are you trying to drive us out of business?"

The words left Annalise's mouth before she'd really thought about them, but now that they'd found voice, she realized she'd just spoken her biggest fear out loud. She knew Luca harbored animosity toward her father, and she didn't blame him. But did he project that same animosity on the casino? She'd questioned his motives from the beginning, but he'd convinced her he was there to help.

Or at least he'd said he was willing to take on the challenge because of Anderson Stone.

After getting off the phone with Mr. Harding, she'd questioned her own intelligence.

"No." Luca's teeth ground together. "Anyone who doesn't understand that every move we make, penny we spend or keyword we google is being logged, cataloged and sold is not thinking clearly. Privacy is an illusion, a reality no one possesses anymore. Everyone is connected and everything is exposed. We blindly give up our privacy in exchange for convenience. And if my questions ripped that rug out from under your precious Mr. Harding, then that's on him. Not me."

Annalise stared at Luca. The expression on his face was clear. He was both irritated and pissed. She'd clearly hit a sore spot with him, which surprised her. And took some of the heat out of her own anger.

What she didn't get, though, was how he could be so clueless when it came to customer relationships. He was a businessman for heaven's sake.

"It isn't your job to open anyone's eyes, Luca. Least of all my customers'. Do not contact them again without my permission or without me being present."

His eyes narrowed. "What good is reviewing these reports if we're not going to question the customers with red flags on their activity?"

Annalise shook her head. "I can't afford to alienate good customers. People talk and you better than most should understand that the casino world is small."

"All the more reason to question people. Maybe they aren't involved or responsible, but maybe they've seen something or someone suspicious."

"Someone that our own security team hasn't found?"

Luca's eyebrows simply rose. Oh, she got his point. Someone had been stealing from the Magnifique for months without notice by her security team. It took routine review of reports to catch the discrepancy. Which was why they ran the reports. And if she hadn't been so hands-on... Annalise didn't want to think about how much longer it could have gone on without being caught.

But that didn't mean it was okay for Luca to act like a TV show cop. "People talk," she said again. "And I can't afford for rumors of issues at the Magnifique to get out. Come up with another way."

Before he could argue with her, Annalise spun on her heel. She needed a break. Striding out of the casino, she jumped into her Range Rover and headed for Excess, her brother's high-end club. She needed to vent and more than likely she'd find her brother and Meredith, her best friend and Dominic's fiancée, there.

The drive was second nature to Annalise and passed by in a blink. When she entered, she bypassed the club, which was just getting busy for the night, and went straight up to the executive offices on the second floor.

Annalise didn't bother knocking at her brother's office door, but came striding in. And she was relieved to see both Dominic and Meredith inside.

Clearly, she was interrupting a hot and heavy kiss, though, because her brother's hands were cupped around Meredith's ass, grinding her body hard against his. Their lips locked together and neither of them even realized she was there until she said "Get a room" and dropped into a chair on the far side of the office.

Dominic growled. Meredith laughed. Her friend turned, a happy sparkle in her eyes even as her hands kept tight hold of the man she loved.

It was good to see them both happy, but at the

same time, the heat smoldering between them made Annalise think of Luca. Not just the irritation he'd caused, but the molten heat from the kiss they'd shared.

She was trying very hard to forget.

"We do have a room. A private office. With the door closed. In case you hadn't noticed," Dominic grumbled.

Meredith smiled up at him. She pressed her lips to his in a quick kiss before pulling back. "Be nice. Annalise clearly needs some help."

"How do you figure?" he asked, glancing over at her with a puzzled expression on his face.

"Because I'm here when I should be at the casino. Because my face is probably going to be permanently wrinkled from the frowning. And because your fiancée clearly knows me better than you do."

She and Meredith had been friends since middle school. She knew all Annalise's secrets, at least the ones she shared with anyone.

Dominic sighed. "You're not going to leave, are you?"

"Not until I get some information."

Dropping his hands from Meredith's waist, Dominic walked across the office and sank onto the couch opposite. Meredith joined him, leaning into his body with an easy familiarity that suggested they sat together often.

An unexpected streak of jealousy shot through Annalise's chest. No, she didn't begrudge her friend and her brother their happiness. In fact, she loved them together. They were perfect for each other. Meredith's calm, cool and focused demeanor balanced out Dominic's hedonistic, wild and carefree nature. Not to mention, they loved each other.

She'd never felt that way about anyone. Ever. There was a part of her that wondered if maybe she just wasn't capable of that kind of emotion. She'd dated. Plenty. But no man had ever been worth sacrificing time at the job she loved. Usually, when she was out, her mind was back at the casino.

There was also the little subject of chaos and upheaval. Relationships often led to messy feelings and drama, which she'd had enough of in her life. Annalise liked things simple, and in her experience, relationships were rarely that.

Besides, it wasn't like she'd grown up with wonderful examples of loving relationships. Her parents had divorced when she was a toddler. Her mother had married an abuser. And the women her father had in his life never stayed long and weren't what she would have called maternal.

"What's going on?"

"What do you know about Luca Kilpatrick?"

Dominic studied her for several seconds before answering. "I know he and Dad have a history. I know he's extremely good at what he does and has done rather well for himself. He's an infrequent guest at Excess, but a VIP every time he comes.

He treats the staff well and doesn't seem to have an ego. Why?"

"Why did Stone recommend him?"

"Because he's damn good at what he does. He has the skills you need and he owed Stone a favor."

"How does Stone know him?"

"I got to know him through Excess and introduced them several years ago. They became friends."

Annalise drummed her fingers against the arm of the chair. Nothing Dominic had said was helpful. Honestly, she wasn't certain what she was hoping to learn, but something. Something to either help her deal with Luca or help her deal with her own response to him.

Meredith moved, dropping into the chair beside Annalise's. "What's going on?"

"He's difficult to work with. He doesn't understand the Magnifique and how we run the business."

"You mean how *you* run the business." Dominic grinned. "Dad hasn't been involved in the day-to-day in a long time. You're the one making the big decisions and have been for a while."

Dominic was right. The Magnifique had been hers for years. In the beginning, she'd consulted her father about major decisions because he had history, knowledge, and she hadn't trusted herself. But it had been a long time since she'd bothered. He'd retired to San Diego and didn't even live in the city anymore. And maybe that's what was bugging her... Luca might not have outright questioned the way she ran her business, but he *had* questioned her by his actions.

Was she being too sensitive about everything?

No, she wasn't.

"Today, he called several of our biggest and best customers and basically harassed them about their playing habits."

Meredith's eyebrows beetled together. "Uh-oh."

"Exactly. I understand why he did it. He's searching for patterns and hoping that in talking with people they'll slip up and reveal something that might help us. But we can't take a list of our best customers and go on a witch hunt. We'll alienate people."

And right now, considering the amount of money they were losing to this thief, they couldn't afford to lose good, long-term customers. They needed every penny they could get.

"He has no regard for building clientele. And clearly no finesse when it comes to customer service. How can the man run a business?"

Dominic laughed. "He doesn't."

"What do you mean? You just said he was wildly successful."

"He is. At creating and building things. At using technology and engineering to solve problems. Stone didn't give you his background?"

"No. No one did." She'd searched the internet, but there wasn't much posted about Luca. Apparently, the walls around his estate weren't the only ones he kept. The man maintained a low profile, which considering what he'd said earlier made much more sense now.

"Luca builds things and sells them to the highest bidder."

"He's out for a quick buck?" Annalise would have believed that statement before, but now, after watching how thorough Luca was when dissecting information, she was skeptical that money was what drove him. Sure, he obviously had plenty, but it wasn't like the job he was doing for her was paying him millions.

"No, actually, he often donates his software and technology to organizations who need the solutions but can't afford to pay for them. I mean, he creates and then he lets someone else deal with the headaches involved in production, marketing, sales and management. He pours blood, sweat, tears and often years of his life into these projects and then walks away once the solution is discovered."

Annalise stared at her brother. She let the information he'd provided filter through her own assessment of Luca. And a few pieces finally clicked.

"He doesn't stick."

Dominic shook his head. "His parents died in a car accident when he was seven. Entered the foster system and bounced from family to family for years. He scored unbelievably high on the SAT and got a full ride to MIT. He's brilliant but detached. I'm no psych major, but my guess is he's gotten burned sometime in the past and just doesn't let people or things become important to him. Because they never stayed."

A heavy weight settled in Annalise's stomach. The picture Dominic painted of Luca's childhood left a pain in her chest. No child should grow up feeling like they weren't wanted. Her own childhood had its share of scars, but at least she always knew her mother and father loved her and wanted the best for her. Even if she didn't always agree with their decisions or methods. And she'd always had Dominic.

Luca was utterly alone.

Annalise thought back to the day she'd crashed his home. That huge mansion and she hadn't seen another soul. Not a housekeeper or assistant. No one but him.

The anger she'd nursed since leaving the casino melted away. Oh, she was still upset with him, but it helped to understand that he truly didn't get what he'd done.

Meredith reached out, covering her hand. "What's really going on between the two of you?"

Annalise blinked. She honestly didn't know how to answer that question. Everything Dominic had just told her should have her running as far away from Luca Kilpatrick as possible. But there was something about him... She just couldn't walk away.

No matter how complicated or messed up things would inevitably become.

"I have no idea."

"But something," Meredith said.

Annalise nodded. She looked over at her brother, expecting to see an angry expression. Instead, his head tilted sideways, and his eyes watched her.

"Tell me this isn't smart," she said. That's what big brothers were for, right? To warn sisters away from guys who were a bad bet?

"I'm the last person you should look to for love advice, Lis. I almost screwed up my chance with the best woman in the world because I was a stubborn ass. I didn't think I was good enough for Meredith."

"Which is the stubborn-ass part," her best friend chimed in, a smile in her voice.

"You don't take risks, Lis, and I better than anyone understand why. You don't trust people easily. You gather them around you and let them confide in you, but you don't put your own thoughts, fears and needs out for consumption. If there's something between you and Luca, then I say you need to at least try. You'll always wonder if you don't."

Dammit, her brother was right.

She did wall herself away from people, letting very few inside. Oh, she put on a good show, but the two people in this room were really her only true, close friends. And until today, she'd never questioned whether that was healthy or smart.

Even men, she held them at arm's length, never really giving them the opportunity to build something with her.

Right now, for the first time in her life, she was wondering if maybe she wanted to.

Six

Luca stared across the casino floor. Annalise had been gone for over an hour, but he knew she'd be back eventually. In the meantime, her words kept running through his head.

He got why she was irritated, and perhaps he shouldn't have made the phone calls to her customers without her awareness. But when there was a problem in front of him to solve, he often operated with blinders on.

He did tend to have a one-track mind. He'd simply thought of a way to gather more useful information. But perhaps there was a way to get what he wanted, while still being mindful of Annalise's customer relations concerns.

The crowd of people around him split to reveal Annalise marching across the casino floor, barreling straight for him.

God, she was gorgeous.

Golden hair swirled around her shoulders. Her chocolate-and-honey eyes flashed fire and her entire body was drawn tight, preparing for a fight.

One he didn't want. Luca didn't want to argue with Annalise. He wanted to love her. To taste and touch her. To hear her moan his name as he buried himself deep inside the warmth of her welcoming body.

But he was smart enough to realize if he tried to touch her right now, she'd take his head off.

"Upstairs. Let's talk."

She didn't bother waiting for his response but brushed straight past him heading for the bank of elevators. Soft music filled the small space, but it wasn't loud enough to cover up the tiny tap, tap, tap of her fingernails against the shiny chrome railing.

He wanted those nails raking down his naked back as he stroked deep inside her.

Seriously, he needed to get his head back on straight or he was about to lose whatever verbal sparring match they were about to enter.

Holding the door to her office open for him, she swept her hand out in a gesture for him to precede her inside. The door closed with a quiet click, and for the briefest of moments, Luca imagined backing her against the closed door and devouring her mouth.

Maybe he should. Maybe the distraction would be good for them both.

He might have done it, but the words that came out of her mouth stunned him and stopped him in his tracks.

"I'm sorry I let my emotions get the better of me earlier. That was unprofessional and it won't happen again."

Wait. She'd left angry because he'd done something to offend one of her customers and she was the one apologizing? "No."

She shook her head, bewildered. "What?"

"No, you don't need to apologize. I shouldn't have called the customers without your approval. I can be like a dog with a bone when I'm working a problem… It's a personal flaw."

He watched as all the fight left her body. Hand still wrapped around the doorknob, she sagged against the office door.

No, that was definitely not the fantasy he'd just fought against. He didn't like seeing her this way. Tired. Overwhelmed. Annalise had too much spirit to be brought low like this.

Without thinking, Luca closed the space between them. He reached for her, pulling her into his arms and offering her the support of his body.

She felt right there.

Her warmth melted into him, spreading slowly through his own skin. At first, her body was stiff, but then she let go. Resting her forehead against the center of his chest, he simply held her.

"Everything will be fine. We'll figure this out."

We'll. It was a simple word, but one he didn't use very often. There was no *we* in his life and never had been. But it had come out without any thought or intention. He wanted to help her, not simply because he'd promised a friend, or because it was an opportunity for a little revenge, or because she'd presented him with a puzzle his brain couldn't let go of. But because she needed *him*, and he wanted to be the one to help her.

With his arms wrapped around her, Luca felt the slow, deep breath that she pulled in. Knew she held it for several seconds before slowly, methodically pushing all the air back out again. She did that several more times, her body relaxing just a little more with each breath.

Eventually, she pushed away and glanced up with a wry smile twisting her lips.

"I've already broken my promise. Sorry."

"Do not apologize to me again, Annalise."

Tucking a strand of hair behind her ear, Luca let his fingers linger as they brushed against the soft texture of her skin. "Let's figure out a solution we can both live with. Since I can't harass your customers."

Annalise punched him, but there was no force behind the blow. "No, you can't harass my customers. What information were you trying to discover, anyway? It's not like the guilty person is likely to come out and tell you what they're doing."

She was right. "No, but they might accidentally give away information that could help."

"And you thought calling them out of the blue, something no one in our office has ever done, wouldn't make them suspicious or cautious?"

Luca grinned down at her. "I'm not that foolish. I possibly implied that the Magnifique was considering implementing a new, highly lucrative program and based on previous history these customers would qualify. And we wanted their opinion."

Annalise shook her head. "Your devious mind is a scary thing sometimes."

"Please." Luca scoffed, "There's nothing devious about my mind."

Annalise's eyebrows rose with disbelief, but she didn't directly respond. "Maybe you're onto something, though."

Pacing away, Annalise walked across the room to the windows that overlooked the strip, but she didn't linger. Instead, she turned on her heel and kept going. He could see the wheels inside her head churning just as quickly as her feet ate up the distance of the floor.

"We need to gather a specific group of customers in one place, right?"

"Yes."

"And while they're here we want to watch their gambling habits and possibly ask a few specific people some questions, right?"

"Watching their habits would actually be better than what I was trying to accomplish with phone calls. Part of the loyalty program involves rewards for those who win, correct?"

Annalise nodded. "Yes."

"So, it stands to reason that the person stealing from you, by artificially prompting the machines to pay out, would be among your high winners."

Annalise paused long enough to run her hand down her face. "In theory."

"But if that person were to play in a large group, where they were aware of being watched, they likely wouldn't receive the same payout percentage."

"True."

"So, let's gather together a targeted set of loyalty customers in a way where we can watch their play and see what happens."

A light of excitement sparked deep inside Annalise's eyes. "We could hold a gala. A thank-you to our most loyal customers. And we *have* actually been thinking about making some changes to the loyalty program. We can use that announcement as an excuse."

Together, they both grinned.

"Perfect."

What had she been thinking?

When she'd thrown out the idea of a gala, she hadn't really thought through the logistics. In order to make it valuable in helping solve the theft, it needed to be thrown together quickly.

It had taken every person on her staff and lots of overtime to pull everything together, but they'd made it.

The last week and a half had been a blur, but tonight they were almost there.

Annalise stared at her reflection in the mirror. The room behind her was bathed in golden light. Through the floor-to-ceiling windows, the stars and moon shone bright enough to be fantasy, not reality. Somehow, the whole night had that feeling wrapped around it. Like an insulating, distorting haze.

For some reason, her stomach churned. Not from concern over what might happen tonight, at least not with the investigation. Anticipation mixed with a little apprehension.

Tension had been building between her and Luca for days. Luckily, the speed with which they'd had to move left no time to act on the need sparking between them. Which only meant the energy had built and built to the point of combustion.

Each time she occupied the same room with Luca, Annalise felt like her skin was going to explode from the force of wanting him. Which was disconcerting. Annalise didn't like not having control of herself or the situation around her. She'd compensated by throwing herself into minute details of this night, making sure it went perfectly.

But now, it was here, and the distraction she'd been using would be gone.

Annalise wasn't certain she was ready for what came next. But it was barreling toward her anyway.

Meredith had helped her pick out her dress. And thank God her friend would also be attending with Dominic. But right now, Annalise was second-guessing her decision of what to wear. When they'd been in the boutique downstairs, enjoying champagne and laughing as they went through the available stock, she'd felt like a million bucks when she'd put it on.

Normally, she dressed fairly conservatively. She needed to do so in order to maintain a professional demeanor. The dress for the gala was a compromise between that professionalism and the sexual energy that had been flooding her blood for weeks.

The skirt was sleek, dropping straight to the floor from her waist in a flowing train. The underskirt matched her light skin tone with an overlay of delicate black mesh and an intricately beaded geometric design. The bodice was black silk, a plunging neckline that left the center of her chest bare almost to the waist. The fabric gathered into narrow straps that crossed her shoulders and met again at the small of her back.

"I'm showing a lot of skin," she murmured.

From out in the living room, Meredith's voice rang out.

"You look gorgeous! Would you stop second-guessing everything? That dress was made for you. It's elegant, sexy and makes a statement."

Annalise wasn't sure she wanted to make a statement tonight.

Meredith stopped in the doorway, leaning against the edge of the jamb. "Luca's going to be struck speechless when he sees you."

Annalise frowned. "I don't care what Luca thinks."

Meredith raised a single eyebrow. "Don't try to bullshit me, Annalise Mercado. I've known you too long for that. You like him. It's okay to admit it."

Internally, she bit back a groan. "Maybe."

"No maybe about it. I've seen the signs before. I know what I'm talking about."

"It's not a good idea. Messy." If she was honest, Annalise would admit that Luca scared her. He was brilliant and sexy. Irritating and dictatorial. He made her want to scream and kiss the hell out of him, often within seconds of each other.

There was nothing easy about Luca Kilpatrick. And the volatile energy that they'd already struck off each other made her uneasy. No, she hadn't seen any evidence of an explosive personality, but she'd hazard a guess neither did her mother until it was too late.

Annalise was aware that she'd gone through life picking men that were safe and comfortable. Which was one reason why none of them particularly mattered.

Luca… He could matter. And he could hurt her, not physically but definitely emotionally.

"Weren't you the woman who advised me just months ago to fight for what I wanted and to go after your brother no matter how messy it might be?"

"That's different."

"Oh, yeah? How?"

Annalise's mouth pulled down at the corners. The real answer was because then she wasn't the one putting anything on the line. "You and my brother are perfect for each other and have wanted each other for years."

Meredith hummed in the back of her throat. "Didn't you say that the first time you laid eyes on Luca, years ago, he was a handsome devil with an attitude problem?"

This was the problem with having a best friend you told everything to. They used it against you later.

"Go and enjoy. Whatever happens." Meredith waggled her eyebrows in a suggestive gesture that had Annalise dissolving into groaning laughter.

The trepidation that had settled in her stomach eased. Squaring her shoulders, Annalise strode out to the elevator and headed down to the ballroom on the casino floor.

Walking through the casino, she glanced around at the patrons. Interspersed between the regular guests were gala attendees decked out in their own finery.

Glitter, silk and satin. Couture gowns and tailored tuxes. Every rainbow of precious gems sparkled around necks, fingers and wrists. The moment reminded her of old Las Vegas, the stories her father and his friends would tell. Glamour and excess. Risk and reward.

Standing in the doorway to the ballroom, Annalise couldn't help the swell of pride as she took in the large room. In just over a week, they'd transformed the space from ordinary to enchanting. From mundane to magical.

Candles sparkled off cut crystal vases filled with a riot of colorful flowers. Black and gold were the perfect backdrop, making the space feel sumptuous and elite.

But it was the man striding toward her, cutting through the crowd like the people didn't exist, that stole her breath.

Annalise was gorgeous and that dress was going to be the death of him. The long skirt clung to her body, swirling around her hips in a way that made her appear to float instead of walk. And the top… The thin fabric clung to her skin, revealing more than it hid, and gave the distinct impression that it might just slither off at any moment.

She was temptation in the flesh. And Luca had to bite back a possessive growl when he caught two men staring at her as she entered the room.

Her golden hair had been pulled up into an elegant upsweep that elongated her neck and throat while wispy tendrils kissed her shoulders. He wanted to bury his lips at her throat and nip at the pulse that skittered just beneath her skin.

Her quick gaze surveyed the room in front of her, cataloging and double-checking details as her mind whirled. Her warm brown eyes flashed with intelligence, confidence and a tiny cut of trepidation.

Her gaze snagged on his and froze. A smile lit her eyes and his stride faltered at the impact. As if someone had punched him straight in the gut.

Reaching her, Luca couldn't stop himself from leaning down and brushing his lips across her cheek. Her skin was soft and the sweet, musky scent of her invaded the air around him.

"You smell better than all the flowers in this room," he murmured into her ear.

She laughed, the quiet sound just for him. Her hand landed on his chest, easing him away. He didn't want to go. His body locked up for several seconds, fighting against her before finally giving in.

Putting a few inches between them, Luca shoved his hands deep into the pockets of his tux. It was either that or wrap an arm around her and tuck her into the shelter of his body. And instinct told him that wouldn't go over very well.

She might look like a dream, but she was here to work. They both were. And Luca needed to remember that.

"What's the plan?" she asked, her gaze running over the growing crowd in front of them. Invitations had gone out to most local cardholders with a certain threshold of spending in the last three years. They'd also extended invitations to a very select group of out-of-state players in the hopes of luring the individuals they wanted to observe.

There were special incentives and rewards for slot machine play, and plainclothes security staff monitoring that area. But they'd also decided it would be smart to implement some additional table games in the main ballroom. A Texas Hold'em tournament that would likely go into the early morning hours. In addition, blackjack, roulette, craps and baccarat.

They'd agreed that he would make his rounds at the tables to see if he could spot anyone cheating. It had been a long time since he'd used his skills at a casino, although counting cards wasn't the kind of ability that got rusty.

Around them, waiters milled with trays of sparkling champagne with berries in the bottom of the glass. Little plates of hors d'oeuvres were available as well. Later, a buffet would be served. They'd discussed not only the cost of a sit-down meal, but also the distraction that kind of dinner would bring. They wanted guests at the tables and slot machines.

But because Annalise was an intelligent businesswoman, and they wanted this event to appear as exactly what they'd billed it, she was going to be opening the evening with a speech. Flipping her wrist over, Annalise glanced at the slim gold watch resting there.

Giving him a brilliant smile, she said, "It's my turn," and then headed off in the direction of the dais and microphone set up at the far end of the room.

The tech team had come up with a phenomenal idea and put together a slide show of pictures of guests. It flashed behind Annalise on a huge screen. Small murmurs would erupt from various sections of the room each time someone recognized themselves.

It was a brilliant way to make everyone feel special and appreciated. The hope was that it also provided a sense of safety so that if the thief was present, they'd feel comfortable taking a risk and making a move during the event.

From his position at the back of the room, Luca watched Annalise. She glided up to the podium and with a soft, welcoming smile gazed out at the crowd. He knew from talking with her that her speech was unprepared and every one of the words of welcome and appreciation that she gave came straight from her heart.

She loved the Magnifique and every single person inside the place. It was something he didn't understand, but also something he envied.

Honestly, he should have been watching the people around him, building information and cataloging details that might be important later. But he couldn't take his eyes off her.

Not only was she gorgeous, but she was dynamic. Breathtaking.

"She's something, isn't she?"

A woman with long red hair and laughing eyes slipped up beside him. He hadn't met Dominic Mercado's fiancée in person, but he knew who she was.

He'd also seen her interviewed on several national news channels over a story she broke about the vice president a couple years ago.

She was cute, and not quite as polished as he'd remembered. And nothing compared to Annalise.

"She is that."

"If you hurt her, I'll hunt you down and murder you."

A surprised laugh blasted out between Luca's smiling lips. "Isn't warning me off something her brother should be doing?"

"Oh, don't worry. I'm sure he'll get around to it. But, honestly, you should probably be more scared of me than of him. He could make you disappear, but I can make your life miserable. His torture would be over quickly...mine wouldn't."

The twinkle in her eyes made it appear that she was making a joke, but there was a glint of something deep behind that sparkle that made Luca think she was serious. If he screwed over Annalise, she'd make his life miserable, and she had the media contacts to do it.

"Trust me, I'm well aware of the Mercado penchant for retribution. Where do you think I got this limp?"

Meredith opened her mouth to say something else, but Dominic appeared by her side and she apparently changed her mind. Her mouth snapped shut.

Dominic reached across his fiancée, offering Luca a hand. "We appreciate your help. I know Annalise has been worried, but you've taken some of that burden off of her. She'll probably never tell you how appreciative she is, but I will."

Luca shrugged. "Don't thank me. I haven't done anything yet."

Around them, a rousing round of applause broke out through the crowd. Annalise spread her arms wide and said, "Please enjoy the evening. There are special contests, prizes, games and tournaments set up through the ballroom and the casino floor. Enjoy, and thank you for being loyal to the Magnifique. We greatly appreciate you being part of our family."

Annalise moved gracefully through the crowd, stopping occasionally to speak to people as she worked her way toward them. A smile on her face, she greeted her brother and friend with a kiss on the cheek.

"This might not be as hedonistic as some of the parties you've thrown, but enjoy yourselves anyway," she said, grinning up at Dominic.

Wrapping her arm through Luca's she gave him a gentle tug. "We're going to go find a table and see what we can discover."

Seven

Annalise watched as Luca played at the various table games. She knew the rules, intimately, but had never been one to enjoy participating. She left that up to him. She blew on his dice at the craps table, cheered as he won several spins of roulette. They'd both agreed he would stay away from the blackjack table.

Now, a couple hours into the party, Luca was seated at one of the poker tables. They'd decided to run a mini tournament. Tables had started in waves and would eventually consolidate as players lost. There was no buy-in, which meant she didn't feel bad knowing Luca had an advantage. The guests were playing for various prizes the Magnifique had offered up as incentive.

Still, there was something about watching Luca that made the blood in her veins sing. He was focused, handsome and damn good.

He'd been playing for almost two hours, watching the various players even as he concentrated on his own game. She'd left him to make her rounds several times, but always found herself back at the table. At some point, he'd shed his tux jacket and rolled the sleeves of his crisp white dress shirt up his muscled arms.

His eyes focused intently, not on the cards, but on the other people at the table. He'd been slow to start. Instead of being aggressive, he'd taken the opportunity to watch the other players, to learn their strengths, weaknesses and tells.

Not that he needed them.

They both knew he was counting the cards and running probabilities in his head each time the dealer flipped a card onto the table.

Annalise had watched as the stack of chips in front of him steadily grew. About an hour and a half in, he'd trapped one of his opponents into playing a hand that he shouldn't. The man had been bragging and talking trash the entire time, running his mouth when he should have been paying attention to the table.

Luca bided his time, watching for the perfect moment to put him out of the tournament. Annalise had half expected Luca to gloat or make some snide comment when he did. Instead, he simply gazed at the man with calm, uncaring eyes, letting everyone around them know he found him inferior.

Systematically, Luca dropped players. Not the ones who were enjoying themselves and polite, but those who didn't deserve to win. Their table was consolidated a couple times until there were about twenty people left.

After several hours in a chair, rarely losing a hand, Annalise watched Luca carefully dispose of all of his chips.

He strategically lost them to people, a mother sitting across from him, a local college student, a retired military veteran. Luca had read the files on everyone at the table and probably knew more about their background than they did. He helped them increase their chip count so they were positioned better for the final round, and then he graciously bowed out.

Annalise had known he intended to lose but watching him do it… He was a brilliant master.

And she'd never wanted him more.

Sure, the man was sexy as hell. And his mind was brilliant. But there was something about watching him purposely lose that had heat building between her thighs and need pulsing just beneath her skin.

And right now, Annalise couldn't remember why she was fighting it.

A wry grin curled his lush lips. "Can't win them all, huh?"

"I guess that depends on what you count as a

win," Annalise said. Grasping his hand, she tugged him along behind her as they melted into the crowd.

Pushing through a door, Annalise pulled him into the back of the house. Spinning, she grasped his shoulders, backed him into the wall and crushed her mouth to his.

She'd stunned him. For the first few seconds he simply stood there, giving everything she demanded. The moment made her feel powerful, sexy. But his passive response didn't last.

Grasping her around the waist, Luca jerked her tight against his body and spun. This time, it was her back that pressed hard against the cold stone of the wall. The rough texture of it scraped against her exposed skin.

She wanted him to kiss her, to take control and flood her body with the delicious sensations she'd been fantasizing about for weeks.

But he didn't. Instead, he simply stood, so close that she could feel the power coiled in his muscles. Other than his arm around her waist, Luca didn't touch her.

And, God, she wanted him to. Hell, she'd practically thrown herself at him. Her body throbbed with a need only he could soothe.

Luca stared down at her, his gaze intense and calm. Part of her resented his control when she felt full of chaos and overpowering need.

Leaning close, he growled, "Be very sure about

this, princess. I've been holding on by a thread and it's about to snap."

Somehow, the confession centered her. She wasn't alone in the storm raging deep inside.

"I'm very sure," she whispered, going up onto her toes and finding his mouth again.

This time she didn't have the element of surprise. And Luca controlled every moment of the kiss. But it wasn't simply that he devoured her, oh, no. She maybe could have retained a semblance of control if he had pushed back and demanded just as much.

Instead, he seduced her with nothing but his lips and tongue. Stroking deep inside her mouth in a way that made a moan float up from the back of her throat. He nipped at the corners of her lips. Nibbled his way across her mouth, sampling all of her and driving her mad.

She wanted more.

But each time she tried to lean forward to take it, the solid pressure of his body held her firmly in place.

Who knew how long they might have stayed there, possibly until he made her beg. But the loud bang of another door down the hallway had them both startling apart.

What was she thinking? Letting him seduce her in the middle of a back hallway? How would that have looked if one of her employees found them?

Pushing him away, Annalise scooted around him. Luca let her go, but only so far. He snagged her arm and held her firmly in place. "No, I won't let you run away again."

Annalise shook her head. She had no intention of running. Her body wouldn't let her. She burned. And what he could give her was the only solution.

Using his hold on her, she tugged at his arm. "Follow me."

Luca let her lead. He was curious to discover where she was going and what she had in mind. That kiss had been…all-consuming, and he wanted more. Much more.

The click of her heels against the bare concrete floor echoed down the hall. They came to a service elevator that he'd never noticed before, although the place was big enough that there were probably plenty of nooks and crannies he hadn't seen yet.

Punching a button, she reached into the bodice of her dress and pulled out a key card. Popping it into a miniscule slot, a light turned green and the car started up.

Annalise was quiet. Her lips were slick and swollen from their kiss. Her eyes glimmered with a heat that Luca felt deep down in his soul.

She wanted him as much as he wanted her, and she was doing nothing to try and hide that fact. No, it was more than that. She stared at him, daring him to see. Elegant and bold, it took everything Luca had not to rip the straps of her dress right off her body and start feasting on her in the elevator.

A loud ding reverberated through the space, followed by the soft hiss of doors as they opened…right into the back of her apartment.

This time she didn't take his hand but strode out and simply expected him to follow. Luca didn't hesitate. And he was rewarded with the most amazing sight when he did.

The hallway in her apartment was lit by soft, golden light. It bathed the silvery gray walls…and the soft velvet of her skin. Reaching behind her, Annalise released the tiny hooks holding the straps to the back of her dress.

Never in his life had he been turned on by the curve of a woman's spine, but just the sight of the long expanse of her naked skin had his erection punching against the unyielding line of his fly.

Long, elegant fingers reached for the zipper that cupped the curve of her ass. Luca swallowed. Hard. The sides fell open revealing nothing but skin. She'd been naked beneath that dress all night.

"Good God, woman. Are you trying to kill me?"

The soft tinkle of her laughter brought out an answering smile.

Glancing over her shoulder, Annalise threw out at him, "My choice in undergarments had nothing to do with you."

"Bullshit." At least he hoped it was bullshit. He liked the idea of her thinking about him as she decided not to put anything between her skin and the dress.

Her arms, crossed just beneath her breasts, were the only thing holding up her dress. With a toss of her head and a challenging smile, Annalise dropped her arms, took two measured steps forward, and let the material slither slowly down her body.

He'd heard people talk about time standing still, but never in his life had he experienced the sensation. Yet in that moment his brain cataloged each miniscule stretch of her body that was revealed as the expensive fabric fell into a puddle at his feet.

Bold as daylight, completely bare except for the four-inch heels on her feet, Annalise walked through the open doorway at the end of the hall.

"Leave the shoes on," Luca growled, his own pace picking up.

She was halfway to the massive platform bed standing in the middle of the room when he caught up to her. Wrapping his arms around her from behind, Luca crushed her back against him.

Annalise sighed, the sound pure relief mixed with anticipation. Her hips rolled, rubbing her ass against the hard ridge of him.

"You're still wearing clothes," she murmured.

"Excuse me for not keeping up."

Rolling her head so she could peer at him out of the corner of her eye, she smirked at him. "You're forgiven."

Turning in his arms, Annalise reached for the buttons of his shirt. Never in his life had the act of unbuttoning a shirt felt like torture. He wanted to brush her slow hands away so he could finish the job himself, but then he'd miss out on the opportunity for her hands against his skin.

Hell would have to freeze over before he'd miss that.

The backs of her fingers stroked down his chest, lower and lower until her fingertips grazed beneath the waistband of his pants.

He let out an involuntary groan when she grazed against the swollen head of his cock. He wanted her to continue to the fly of his pants. Instead, she pulled her hand away, wrenching another noise from his throat.

Reaching for his shirt, Annalise spread it wide, sweeping it down his shoulders and off onto the floor. Leaning forward, she placed her mouth to his skin and sucked. The tiny pinprick of her teeth nibbled across his chest until she found the flat disc of flesh and tugged on the nub in the center. A spike of need shot straight down to his groin.

"Ever since that day you walked out on your front porch, rumpled, sleepy and grumpy, I've wanted to taste your skin."

The confession shouldn't have had the blood whooshing even faster in his veins, but it did.

And he realized he was a fool for standing there, her naked body just waiting for him, while she played.

Reaching for her, Luca filled his palms with the soft, round mounds of her breasts. Leaning down, he laved his own tongue across the tight bud of flesh and relished her soft whimper. Sucking her breast into his mouth, Luca savored the salty, sweet taste of her as it bloomed against his tongue.

God, he'd wanted her for what felt like forever. And now that he had her...Luca almost wasn't sure what to enjoy first. It was the overwhelming sensation of a kid at his first amusement park. So many choices.

Wrapping his hands around her waist, Luca boosted her up into his arms. Her long legs wrapped around his body, ankles digging into the small of his back. Her body burned as her naked skin slid against his.

Three giant steps had his knees touching the edge of her bed. Tipping her back, he let her fall onto the mattress behind her.

Annalise scrambled up onto her elbows, reaching for him even as he stepped away. Her golden blond hair was a cloud around her face, the ends curling temptingly around the generous curves of her breasts. Her olive skin glowed in the muted moonlight.

She wasn't a princess; she was a goddess. And he fully intended to worship her tonight.

Dropping to his knees, Luca pressed his palms to the inside of her thighs, urging her to open.

An expectant sigh whispered through her parted lips as she complied. Her sex glistened with the evidence of her desire for him, swollen, pink and just begging for his touch.

Spreading her lips, Luca wasted no time diving in for a taste. Sweet and salty, the delicious flavor of her flooded his mouth. It wasn't enough. Over and over, his tongue teased the opening of her body.

His teeth found the tight bud of nerves and gently held it in place while the tip of his tongue swiped over and over again.

Every muscle in her body tightened beneath his onslaught.

She writhed, but Luca held her right where he wanted her. Using his hands to cup her hips, he held her firmly in place. She bucked against his mouth, whimpering even as the pressure built higher and higher.

Her muscles pulsed and fluttered. Her breath sobbed in and out of her lungs.

"Luca." She breathed the single word. He wasn't sure if it was a benediction or a warning, not that it particularly mattered.

"Let me have it, Annalise. Let go." He wanted to claim her orgasm. To feel the moment as she finally let everything free.

And he wasn't disappointed.

Her cry echoed against the ceiling. Her hips thrust against his mouth. Her hands, which had somehow found their way into his hair, clenched so hard his scalp tingled at the violent tug.

Luca rode out the waves of her orgasm, using

his tongue against her clit to pull every last speck of pleasure out of her. She bucked against him, his name a sob on her lips.

When she was done, her body finally spent and silent, Luca crawled up onto the bed beside her.

He watched her as the world finally returned. Her eyelids fluttered for several seconds before opening. Her gorgeous chocolate-and-honey eyes were unfocused at first, but slowly began to zero in on him.

A satisfied smile stretched his face. He couldn't help it. Annalise was so…perfect. Calm, cool, collected. She was always put together and in control.

Right now, in this moment, she was none of those things. And he liked this side of her a whole hell of a lot.

Her hair was a tangled mess, spread out across the rumpled comforter. Occasionally, her body would shiver with the aftereffects of the orgasm he'd just given her.

Never in his life had Luca felt so…empowered after watching a woman come.

Reaching for her, Luca tangled his hand into the strands of her silky hair and used the hold to bring her mouth to his. The kiss was slow and easy. It felt right, like somehow he needed to thank her for opening herself to him the way that she had.

But it didn't stay that way long.

She might be satisfied, but he was far from it. The throb in his cock was overwhelming and insistent.

As if sensing the growling animal of his need, Annalise pushed against his shoulder. Rolling with the nudge, his shoulders hit the mattress and bounced.

She perused him, her gaze moving slowly down his body. She was unhurried and unapologetic about the way she appreciated him. His chest, abs, thighs and especially the long length of his cock.

Luca didn't much care about how he looked. Honestly, he never thought about it. He spent time in the gym because he liked the challenge and because after spending hours in front of a computer, his body needed the physical activity. But right now, the appreciation in her eyes made him feel ten feet tall and bulletproof.

And the wicked gleam in her eyes... It should have scared him. Instead, it only made him want her more.

Eight

Annalise let her gaze travel down Luca's body.

The man could have been the model for a Greek statue. It wasn't fair, how perfect his body was. How strong and capable beneath the well-worn jeans and business suits.

She'd already had a glimpse of him that day at his place, but now…she had an up-close-and-personal view. Clearly, he did more than sit in front of a computer screen all day.

But it was more than just the tight muscles packed onto his frame. Aside from the slight limp, Luca moved with a fluid grace that said he was totally in control of his body.

Somehow, that was sexy as hell.

He'd given her one of the best orgasms of her life, and still, her body hummed with an insistent need.

She wanted more of him.

Folding his hands behind his head, Luca lounged back against the pale blue comforter on her bed. "Look all you want, princess."

The grin on his face was more than just temptation. It was a challenge. Was she going to take what he'd given her and hide, or was she going to follow through and commit to what was happening between them?

Oh, there was no way she was going anywhere.

"Trust me, I plan to do more than look."

Raising a single eyebrow, Luca silently challenged her.

It was always that way between them. A little edge to everything, even this. Somehow, that tension only made her want him more, the bastard.

Annalise reached for him, letting her fingertips slip featherlight across his skin. The rounded curve of his shoulders. The swell of his pecks. The flare of his hips. She played and learned, watching the telltale widening of his eyes when she hit a particularly sensitive spot on his body.

She didn't purposely tease, but that was the result of what she was doing. Annalise had no idea how long she explored, it could have been two minutes or twenty. But the way his muscles tightened beneath her touch fascinated her.

And the longer she did it, the tighter the coil of his body wound.

She wondered when he'd snap. At what point would he reach the end of his rope?

A delicious shiver skated down her spine. Finally, she reached for the jutting line of his sex that she'd been ignoring.

A sharp hiss slipped through his lips, but his hands didn't move from their position behind his head.

Slowly, Annalise let her fingers trail down the hard press of him before wrapping him in the tight grip of her fist. He was silk over steel, hard and soft at the same time. Her thumb played across the tip of him, swiping up the tiny pearl of moisture that leaked out.

She wanted to taste him.

The thought had barely crossed her mind before she was leaning down to pull him deep into her mouth.

His hips bucked beneath her and she thought that might be the moment he broke. But he didn't. Instead, he let her torture him even more. Slowly, she sucked the length of him in until the tip hit the back of her throat. And then she went back up again. Over and over, slow and steady, until her own mind was only focused on the taste and feel of him.

Annalise's eyes closed and her own body burned. She wanted him buried deep between her thighs. To feel the heavy weight of him pinning her to the bed.

Maybe she made a sound—it certainly reverberated through her head—but that was the moment Luca exploded.

The world spun and then her back hit the mattress once again.

Her eyes blinked open to find him staring down at her, the most intense, all-consuming, heated expression she'd ever seen stamped across his face.

"You're mine," he growled.

And all Annalise could do was nod.

"Condom."

Annalise waved a hand to the bedside table, and luckily, he understood what she meant. In record time, Luca had the foil packet ripped open and the ring of latex spread down the long shaft of his sex.

Hand gripping her ankle, Luca wrapped her leg around his waist. His hips pressed into hers, opening her wide. His fingers slipped through the evidence of her desire as he found her opening and then thrust inside.

Annalise's eyes slid shut again at the overwhelming sensation of pleasure bombarding her. It was too much. Not enough.

"Look at me," he demanded. And there was nothing inside her capable of ignoring him.

In and out, he thrust just as slowly as she had been torturing him. And in that moment, Annalise realized she'd been teasing them both.

Luca's face pulled tight, his features sharpened with control and need. Those soul-stealing, stormy eyes stared into her. So deep. The way he looked at her made her feel utterly naked and exposed. Annalise felt the need to cover herself, not her body but her soul. Unfortunately, she didn't know how.

And before she could do something else, like push him away, another orgasm hit.

It came out of nowhere, no warning or preparation. The world spun on its axis, leaving her disoriented, breathless and pulsing with a pleasure she'd never experienced before.

People said sex could be earth-shattering. Until that moment, Annalise had always thought people were lying.

Luca's orgasm swiftly followed on a guttural growl that sent shivers down her spine. She felt the pulse of his release deep inside her body and relished the sensation. Wrapping her arms around him, Annalise hung on to him. His hips thrust against hers several times before he collapsed onto the bed beside her.

His sharp, uneven breaths gushed across her clammy skin. His face buried into the crook of her neck and half of his weight pressed her against the bed.

Her body hummed, with energy, satisfaction and exhaustion. It was the most amazing sensation she'd ever had.

Luca let his fingers slip across Annalise's naked skin. For some odd reason, the easy, comfortable way she lounged naked in bed with him was surprising. He'd half expected her to kick him out of her bed the minute they'd both gotten off and pretend like their night together hadn't happened.

Because that's what he was used to. Being dismissed, unneeded, used.

But Annalise wasn't that way. She'd made a decision to give in to what was between them and from that moment there was no looking back. No regret or second thoughts.

He envied her that certainty. It was something he hadn't found until much later in life. There was nothing quite like being ignored, passed over and unwanted to make someone feel like less of a person. No matter how much you achieved, it was never enough. Because there was no one in your life to confirm that it was. Or tell you they were proud of what you'd accomplished.

Luca shook the thoughts away. They didn't belong in this space and time. Not right now and not with her.

Instead, he let his fingers glide through the soft strands of her hair. His fingertips tingled as they drew lazy patterns across her skin.

She did the same, her gorgeous face relaxed and her eyes half-lidded with drowsy contentment.

He'd given that to her. Pride swelled in his chest.

"Tell me something about you that I don't know," Annalise murmured, her voice quiet and easy just like the muted moonlight that spilled across her body.

Luca shrugged. He always hated those kinds of questions. He never knew what the other person was searching for, because they were always looking for something specific.

"When I was little, potential parents would ask me the same thing. Or some version of it. Tell us about yourself. What do you like to do for fun? I was probably nine or ten when I realized what they were really asking for was evidence that I'd fit neatly into their world. Or more likely for reasons why I wouldn't."

Beneath his head, Annalise's chest rose and fell on a deep breath. Her fingers, painting patterns across his shoulder, paused before starting up again. But she didn't say anything. There were no apologies or empty platitudes to try and make his crappy childhood better. Which he appreciated, because nothing she said could change the past.

"Apparently, understanding that didn't much matter because none of them ever decided to keep me. They always chose someone else. A little girl with pretty hair. Or the younger boy who loved baseball. I was never much into sports. I was smart, but had trouble concentrating in school. Most of the things they were trying to teach us were boring. I much preferred to spend the time researching things on my own."

A soft chuckle melted through her lips. "Always independent, huh?"

Luca shrugged. "I suppose. I'm not sure if that's who I am or if that's what my circumstances created. It doesn't really matter."

"No, maybe not in the broader sense. You are who you are."

"A demanding, unbending asshole?"

Annalise shook her head. Luca felt the movement more than he saw it. "A brilliant, difficult, damaged, sexy and kind man."

"Damaged, huh?"

"We're all damaged, Luca. It's just that some scars are a little more visible than others."

The sadness and exhaustion in her voice surprised him. His stomach clenched because her tone made him certain she knew exactly what she was talking about. And for some inexplicable reason, he wanted her to be one of the very few who weren't damaged. Not because it made life messy, but because he didn't want that for her.

He also wanted to understand her, but it would be rude to ask her to explain. With anyone else, he wouldn't have cared and would have simply voiced the question because he wanted the answer. But with Annalise… She made him want to be better.

Which was both surprising and concerning at the same time.

"Well, I'm fully aware of my scars, visible and invisible. I've been through plenty of therapy and understand the reasons I am the way that I am. It took some work, but I'm comfortable with myself."

"That's rather obvious," Annalise answered, her words full of dry humor.

Luca rolled up onto an elbow and glared at her. "What are you implying?"

"Absolutely nothing. I'm pretty sure my comment is transparent. Your ego is the size of Texas, Luca Kilpatrick. However, you also have plenty of reasons for that so it's difficult to fault you. It is occasionally annoying, though."

"Oh, I imagine it is."

Twisting his body, Luca shifted his position so he could cross his arms over her belly and set his chin on his hands to look at her.

He wanted to see her face.

"There's something about you that's very open and appealing, did you know that?"

Annalise huffed. "I'm sure there are plenty of people who would disagree with you."

"Then they're not paying attention. Every single thought you have telegraphs through your body and face."

She shook her head. "You're just good at watching people."

"Maybe. Another skill from my childhood."

The humor on Annalise's face slipped away. "That's a skill we share. My stepfather was abusive. Not to me, but to my mother. I learned quickly to read his expressions and body language for signs that things were getting dangerous. Dominic and I both would do whatever we could to try and defuse the situation. Sometimes it worked. More often, it didn't."

Goddammit.

In his world, he knew plenty of children who'd been in abusive situations. Those scars ran deep.

"Your father didn't kick his ass?"

"My father didn't know until it was too late. My stepfather was quite adept at only letting people see what he wanted them to. He was careful about where he put the bruises on my mom. Dominic and I were young enough that he intimidated us to keep quiet, and we absolutely believed his threats."

"You were scared."

"Rightly so, considering he murdered my mom."

This time, Luca didn't bother to hold the swear word in.

"I've been through plenty of therapy of my own and worked through most of the damage from my childhood. I still harbor anger and guilt sometimes, but not nearly as much as I used to."

"I hope your stepfather is rotting in prison."

A grimace twisted Annalise's lips. "He isn't. It's a long story, but to keep it short, Dominic and I were the only witnesses. My stepfather was a prominent man in the community with lots of friends. And we were just kids. By the time the cops were finished questioning us they'd twisted our story to the point we couldn't be used as witnesses."

Holy hell. Each time Luca thought Annalise's story couldn't get any worse, somehow it did. She'd been young, traumatized and let down by the system that should have helped her seek justice.

In that respect, Luca felt a kinship with her.

He marveled at her strength. Most people would be bitter, but there was none of that in Annalise's voice. In fact, as he watched her expression, Luca realized just how calm and collected she appeared. Sure, there was emotion behind her words—he'd be worried if there wasn't—but it was clear to him that she really had worked through the trauma of what she'd experienced.

It didn't possess or define her. Obviously, it affected her life and had some impact on who she was as an adult. But there was so much more to her than that experience.

Some of what he was thinking must have shown on his face—he'd have to work on that around her. He didn't like to be vulnerable, especially not with Annalise. He'd already given her more of himself than he'd ever shared with anyone else—because she said, "Oh, don't worry. When Dominic got old enough, he made sure the asshole paid. You know a few of our friends. My stepfather systematically lost everything. The last I heard, he was penniless and begging friends for a spare bedroom."

As far as Luca was concerned, that wasn't enough. In that moment, he had the irrational desire to physically harm the man for what he'd done and the trauma he'd caused Annalise. Never in his life had he felt such a visceral response to someone else's pain.

It wasn't logical, which bothered him.

But not enough to get up and leave.

"I'm sorry you experienced that."

Annalise shook her head. As she ran her fingers through his hair, Luca couldn't help but groan and stretch into her touch. A tingle of awareness prickled across his scalp, starting a cascade of response.

"No, I didn't tell you because I wanted your pity. Not only do I not need it, but nothing that happened is remotely your fault."

"Then why did you tell me?"

"Because you implied that having a family and the appearance of everything meant that my childhood was perfect. And I'm absolute proof that looks can be deceiving. Trauma isn't a race to be won or something to be weighed and measured. The trauma you experienced is just as real and devastating as what I experienced, in different ways. But it still affects our lives."

Her fingers stilled, but she stared straight into him as she said, "I don't trust easily, and I'd hazard a guess neither do you."

She was right, but it didn't take much to figure that out. He'd acknowledged that about himself a long time ago.

"My words were twisted and used against me. I felt utterly helpless during that time, frustrated and useless." Annalise looked away, but he could see the intensity and discomfort in her expression. She didn't like recalling the past any more than he did. "I've worked hard not to ever feel that way again, making decisions solely to avoid situations and people, to ensure my life is easy, consistent and predictable.

But right now, this situation with the casino is starting to feel the same way. And it's ripping away the illusion I've built for myself."

Luca dragged his gaze away from her. Watching her emotions right now made him feel…too much.

Responsibility. The sensation of failure, something he hadn't experienced in a very long time. He'd started this job with the Magnifique with…less than pure intentions. Certainly, he intended to do his job and solve the problem, but he'd also planned to exact a little revenge and enjoy watching the Mercado princess squirm.

Now he truly wanted to find the thief. And not because he'd become intrigued, although he had. But because it mattered to Annalise.

And she mattered to him.

Luca had no idea when it had happened, but sometime in the last few weeks what she needed and wanted had become important to him. He knew the stress she was under, had seen the evidence of it himself during their long days and nights of trying to find the needle buried among the haystacks.

Tonight's gala hadn't borne any fruit. Unless there was footage security hadn't scrubbed yet that revealed something, no one they'd earmarked had given any signs of being the thief. But they'd keep looking.

Reaching for her, Luca tugged until she slid down in the bed. He rolled them both so she was tucked beneath him, nothing more than the thin sheet tangled between them.

She stared up at him, her eyes full of frustration and fear. That expression made his belly clench and for some strange reason a promise he wasn't sure he could keep poured out of his lips.

"We'll find the thief, Annalise. I promise."

Nine

Luca stared at the screen. The list of numbers and names blurred. Blinking, he squeezed his eyes shut and opened them again, righting the lines.

Annalise's office was dead silent. But that was to be expected in the middle of the night. He finally understood why she was a workaholic… When you lived and worked in the same space it was too easy to just slip back down to take care of something. And just a few minutes could easily turn into several hours.

He was here in her office because he hadn't been able to sleep. Not an unusual occurrence in his life, considering his sleep pattern was really more of a chaotic jumble.

Annalise's soft, even breathing had been hypnotic and tempting. He'd wanted to curl up beside her and sink down into sleep with her warmth tucked against his body. But his mind wouldn't let him rest. Not when their conversation had renewed his determination to find her thief.

The gala had been disappointing at best. Well, aside from seeing Annalise in that killer dress. That had been worth the effort and preparation alone.

The memory of her standing on that stage, lights bathing her in a golden glow, made his cock throb all over again. If he was smart, he'd shut down the spreadsheet he was looking at, go back upstairs and wake her up for round two.

Luca groaned, the sound breaking eerily through the silence.

Instead, he picked back up where he'd left off, trying to find more anomalies in the data they'd already crunched several times.

By the time weak sunlight filtered into the room his eyes were gritty, his lower back throbbed and his head ached.

But he'd found something.

"So this is where you snuck off to."

Annalise's voice startled him. His gaze jerked up to find her standing in the office doorway, arms crossed, hip and shoulder propped against the jamb.

He half expected to see irritation shining in her gorgeous eyes. But instead, all he read there was curiosity. Most women would have been pissed to wake up alone the morning after sex. Apparently, not Annalise.

Which just proved how unique she was.

And because he didn't want her to think he was avoiding her, Luca didn't bother to respond with words. Instead, he rose from the chair, slowly circled her desk and crossed the room to her. Wrapping his hand around the base of her neck, Luca pulled her mouth to his.

Heat swirled between them. Desire, dormant for the last few hours, stampeded through his system.

She was like a drug, his body immediately responding to the hit.

Her arms dropped to his waist, grasping him and jerking him tight against her own body.

They were both panting by the time he finally pulled away.

"Good morning," he murmured.

"It is now," she responded.

A half grin tugged at the corner of his lips. For some reason, hearing her say those words in that pragmatic and practical tone made him want to laugh.

"How long have you been down here?"

"Almost all night."

She shook her head. "And you accuse me of being a workaholic. At least I sleep."

"That's it, make snide jokes. But I think I found something."

Annalise straightened. She looked at him with a tiny kernel of hope in her eyes. "Really?"

"Yeah. At least something that sticks out as suspicious. We filtered the data and targeted people with an unusual pattern of activity. We assumed, and maybe incorrectly, that considering the volume of loss the thief would have transactions above a certain threshold. But then I remembered that in the beginning, the amounts were actually rather small."

Annalise nodded, following along silently with his logic. Her entire body was strung tight, braced for the impact of what he was saying.

"What if there isn't a single person, but multiple people, involved?"

Tilting her head, she studied him for several moments. He could see the wheels in her brain spinning on the ramifications of what he'd just suggested.

"You mean, there's a ring? Like a group of card counters working together?"

"Something like that. What if multiple people are in on the action, spreading the stolen amounts between loyalty accounts? I filtered for accounts, using probability, that consistently won higher than the expected average but hit amounts below the automatic review threshold."

"Flying under the radar."

"Exactly. It would become obvious if a single person, or a group of people, was constantly showing up on reports. But under the threshold, you could rack up a lot of wins without anyone really noticing."

"Especially if those wins are spread between people."

It was Luca's turn to nod. "Exactly."

"I'm assuming you have a list."

This time, there was nothing halfway about his smile. "Of course I do."

Annalise followed him around the desk to the spreadsheet sitting open on the desktop.

"It's pretty long at the moment—roughly two hundred names. But I'm running some algorithms right now. We should have it narrowed down in a little while."

Annalise's eyes raced across the screen. Impatience pulled her lips into a tight line as she turned to him.

Wrapping an arm around her waist, he tugged her back against his body and murmured in her ear, "I'm pretty sure I can think of a distraction to pass the time."

Waking alone had been a punch to the gut. One Annalise had been determined not to let Luca know he'd landed. Before coming downstairs, she'd convinced herself that there was nothing but chemistry between them.

Which was utter bullshit.

Right now, even knowing that the computer could spit out a list of names which included the thief she'd been tracking for months, she wanted nothing more than what Luca was offering.

Mind-blowing sex.

God, the man made her feel things.

Spinning in his arms, it was her turn to back him up against the sharp edge of the desk.

"Is that right? What exactly were you thinking? Maybe reaching beneath my skirt and pulling my panties down around my ankles?"

Annalise reached for the prominent bulge behind the fly of his jeans. "Maybe bend me over the desk and thrust your cock deep inside me?"

Luca let out a groan, closing his eyes for a moment as if praying for control. His eyes popped open, spearing her straight through with that unforgiving gray. How could she be the one sandwiching him between the desk and her body, but still feel like the one being caught?

"I was actually thinking more about slipping back upstairs to your apartment—see, having work and home so close does have perks—but you've convinced me your idea is better."

She half expected him to reach beneath her skirt, rip the panties from her body and haul her across the desk. And she'd be lying if she didn't admit the idea thrilled her.

Instead, Luca eased her away as he dropped to his knees. He stared up at her, an earnest expression on his face. Slowly, deliberately, he ran the pads of his fingers up her legs from ankles to calves to thighs.

A shiver rocked her body and goose bumps followed his path.

It was pure torture, knowing exactly what he was about to do, waiting for him to fully touch her.

His fingertips grazed her inner thighs, slowly painting circles across her skin. He teased the crease at the apex of her thighs, skimming just beneath the edge of her panties.

Within minutes, she was breathless with need. Burning. Desperate. She didn't even recognize her own voice when she finally said, "Touch me."

His lips quirked up and a triumphant light burst from his intent gaze.

"My pleasure."

Crooking his fingers, Luca snagged the edge of her panties and dragged them inch by excruciating inch down her legs. He gently picked up each of her feet, freeing them.

She was surprised when instead of tossing them onto the floor, he tucked them into the pocket of his jeans.

"I'm going to want those back."

"I'm sure you will, but you're not getting them. They're mine now."

Annalise let out a startled huff. "I can't walk around all day without underwear."

Luca's grin turned perfectly wicked. "Oh, I think you can."

She'd barely registered what he was saying before her mind fractured again when his fingers found the center of her sex and stroked. He'd done it on purpose. Distracted her. The man was sneaky and brilliant, but that was something she'd already known.

Annalise let out a sigh of pleasure. "Do that again," she ordered.

Luckily, Luca was happy to oblige. Fingers wrapped around her outer thigh, he guided her around until her hips hit the edge of the desk. It was a relief to let the furniture take some of her weight… Her knees were less than steady right now.

Luca pressed on her thighs, silently demanding that she open for him. Annalise glanced up, her gaze snagging on the clear glass in the door to her office. It was early, but that didn't mean someone couldn't come wandering in at any moment. The casino was open 24/7.

With any other man, at any other time, that thought would have had her pumping the brakes. In this moment, she didn't care if someone saw them.

No, she wanted someone to see them. To know just how desperate he was for her, and she for him. That shared need made her feel powerful, in a way running a multimillion dollar business never had.

Reaching down, Annalise gathered the tight pencil skirt in her fingers. She slowly walked the hem up her thighs, freeing herself from the restriction until she could widen her stance.

Luca watched her, his eyes glowing with approval and need. His fingers followed the expanse of skin that she revealed. But it was his mouth that did her in.

The minute her skirt revealed the juncture of her

thighs, Luca swooped in. He spread the lips of her sex wide and swiped his tongue through the slit in one long, slow, savoring lick.

Her arms trembled where they propped her body up. Over and over, his tongue teased her. Luca found the tiny nub of nerves and sucked it into his mouth. Holding it softly with his teeth, he used the wicked tip of his tongue to swipe over and over and over again.

Until she saw stars.

Heat ran rampant through her, building and building until it finally exploded. Her body arched up into the waves of pleasure, silently seeking more.

Annalise's arms failed her and she collapsed back onto the desk. Luca took advantage by surging up and pushing her along the solid surface.

She blinked, her mind sluggish even as she watched him make quick work of the fly on his pants. Pulling a condom from a pocket, he rolled it down over the long, pulsing shaft of his sex.

How could she have experienced one of the best orgasms of her life just minutes before and still want more? How was it always this way with him?

It didn't matter. Right now, what did matter was how much she wanted him.

Wrapping his hands around her hips, Luca pulled her to the edge of the desk and positioned his cock at the wet, swollen entrance to her sex. She lifted her hips, an invitation and a demand all in one.

He held her steady as he thrust deep inside. Annalise let out a cry of relief. "More, more, more."

She reached for his hips, urging him faster. Her back arched up off the hard surface of the desk as the band of tension tightened inside her again.

Luca let out a groan before thrusting deep one last time. His entire body shuddered with the force of his climax. Her own body reacted, vaulting into another orgasm that robbed her of everything but the drowning sensations of pleasure.

They both lay there, Luca's body draped across hers and pinning her to the furniture. Small details filtered through the haze. The slide of his legs against hers. The sound of the air-conditioning whooshing on. The way his chest rose and fell on deep, even breaths.

Luca stirred, but for some strange reason Annalise tightened her arms around his prone body, holding him close for a few seconds more before finally letting go.

A feeling of disappointment and anxiety stirred through her belly when he shifted away. Picking her up by the waist, Luca set her on the floor and straightened her clothes for her. He smoothed the hair away from her face and gazed down.

His expression was…enigmatic. She had no idea what he was thinking. What did he want?

What did she want?

Annalise wasn't used to this. Wasn't used to caring.

And staring up into his inscrutable gaze, she realized she did. Care.

She opened her mouth to say…something, but was cut off by a loud ding coming from the computer across the room.

A sardonic smile touched his lips. "My algorithm's finished."

Luca turned away from her, straightening his own clothes.

And just like that, they were back to business.

It took everything inside him not to haul Annalise back against his body. But that wouldn't be good for either of them.

Soon, people would start to arrive at the office to begin their morning. And Annalise would never forgive herself—or him—if they got caught in the act by her staff. She would see that as being irresponsible.

So he walked across the office, tapped a few keys and called up the list that his program had pulled from the database.

Annalise followed behind him. She leaned close as he worked. The honey-and-sin scent of her enveloped him, at once firing him up and settling something deep inside him.

He began scrolling through the data, filtering and condensing it even more as he went. After several minutes, he sat back in his chair and looked at a list of about twenty or thirty names.

"Any of these jump out at you?"

He honestly hadn't expected for Annalise to have

a response. These were people who either flew under the radar because they weren't very good gamblers or because going unnoticed was what they were trying to do. There likely had been no reason for Annalise to interact with any of these people during their visits to the casino.

So he was surprised to see shock cross her face as her eyes scanned furiously through the list. Her mouth thinned and her eyes narrowed. She glanced surreptitiously at him, but he was staring straight at her and noticed the gesture.

She didn't want to tell him.

"Annalise," he said, the single word a warning.

With a sigh, she took several steps back. "It doesn't mean anything."

He had no idea what she was talking about, but he didn't necessarily need to. "Maybe not, but what if it does?"

She shook her head. "It's simply a coincidence. You said yourself this is an algorithm that pulls data. There are lots of names on this list and most of them are probably innocent of any wrongdoing."

Hope and fear mixed deep in her eyes. Luca realized she was really and truly shaken by the name she'd seen. She wanted the person to be innocent, because if they weren't it would be a complete and utter betrayal.

Which would devastate her.

Hell.

"Who is it?" Luca asked, the question grim and

gentle because logic had told him from the very beginning that this was an inside job and they might just have found the connection.

With a sigh, Annalise reluctantly answered. "A former employee. Robert worked for the Magnifique for thirty years. He has an exemplary record and I know him personally. He couldn't be behind this."

For her sake, Luca hoped she was right. But the churning in the bottom of his gut said she wasn't.

He'd need to approach this very carefully. Luca had already run afoul of Annalise's protective instincts when it came to her employees and the family mentality she'd built around them. This was no doubt a man she'd known for her entire life and someone she trusted.

"Fair enough. I trust your judgment, but even you have to admit that since his name is on this list, we need to treat him like all the others."

Annalise swallowed, her throat working for several seconds before she finally nodded. "What do you suggest?"

Ten

Annalise didn't want to believe Robert was involved. No, she *refused* to believe he was involved. But she understood the point Luca had made. In order not to appear biased, they needed to allow for the possibility that she was wrong.

Even if that thought had a pit the size of Texas forming in her belly.

"Before we jump to any conclusions, let's take a look at the camera footage."

Annalise braced for an argument, but after a few seconds Luca nodded his head in agreement. "We can do that."

"Great." Suddenly, the cloud of doom that had gathered above her head began to dissipate. The footage would prove Robert was innocent. That simply had to be the case.

Luca took a step back. "I want to check a couple more things. Why don't you head up to security and ask them to pull the files so we can scrub them?"

That was fine with her. She needed a few minutes to herself, anyway. Between the amazing orgasm and the shock to her system from seeing Robert's name on that list…she was feeling off-center, and that bothered her.

Walking through the casino, she headed to the heart of their security hub, the eye in the sky. It really wasn't that anymore, although the room did have one-way glass that overlooked the casino floor. However, most surveillance was done by cameras and video these days. And the team members patrolling the floor in plain clothes and uniforms.

Walking into the room, several people spun to look at her. Giving everyone a wave and a hello, Annalise headed for the office at the far end. Walking inside, she closed the door behind her before sitting down across from the huge desk that occupied at least half of the space.

"Nick, do we have a way to pull video footage based on player card information?"

Her head of security rocked back into his chair, furrowing his eyebrows as he gripped the arms. His body moved, slowly, a leisurely back-and-forth that she knew from experience was part of his thinking process.

Nick had been with the Magnifique for almost fifteen years. He'd worked his way up the security department to the head spot for the last six. He was thorough, quick under pressure and took his job very seriously.

He also had a beautiful wife, three grandsons and a German shepherd that was his baby.

"We don't tag and catalog footage that way."

Annalise already knew this but wanted to ask the question anyway.

"What are you trying to find?"

"We've identified a group of cardholders with a series of wins just below the standard review level. Before we dig further, I was hoping we could use previous footage to review their habits."

There was no reason to mention to Nick that Robert was on the list. They weren't exactly friends, but they knew each other. Most of the staff were familiar with each other, even if they worked in different departments. And Nick had processed Robert out when he retired a year and a half ago.

Nick's mouth pursed. The quiet click of the door opening behind her interrupted whatever he was about to say. Annalise spun in her chair to see Luca.

Closing the door, he crossed the space and stopped just behind and to her left. The warmth of his hand landed on her shoulder, squeezing for just a moment before dropping away. The gesture was quick, but Nick's eyebrows rose up in surprise anyway.

He was smart enough not to say anything, though.

Annalise wasn't certain how to feel about the gesture. On one hand, the show of support was nice. But on the other, she wasn't exactly used to public displays of affection. Especially at work.

Although, that hadn't exactly stopped her from having sex in her office this morning.

Which had been amazing.

Shaking her head, Annalise tried to return her focus to the task at hand and not the exciting, confusing, sexy man standing just behind her.

"Nick was just about to tell me whether we could filter the video files based on customer loyalty information."

Behind the desk, Nick slowly shook his head. "We just don't catalog the files that way."

"We could run it through facial recognition software," Luca suggested.

"Yes, you're talking about over a year of footage. Even the fastest programs are going to take some time."

Annalise frowned. "Especially when our list of people is over twenty long."

Nick grunted. "We'll set it up, but it's not going to be a fast process."

"We don't need fast. We need accurate," Luca said, his voice holding a grim tinge that didn't give her the warm and fuzzies.

Even he wasn't hopeful that this process would work.

"Let's also flag each of the players on the list. I

want to know if any of them walk through the front door."

Nick nodded, his face clearing just a little. "That we can do."

Well, it was something. Until the program ran or one of the players walked through the door, they were playing a waiting game.

"Thanks for your help, Nick."

"No problem, Annalise. I know this has been a frustrating process and I want to help catch this person just as much as you do."

Standing up, Annalise reached across the desk and set her on Nick's arm. "I know you do."

Turning, she walked back out of the office and through the security hub. Luca matched her pace, his normally long stride modulated to keep up with her.

Once they were out in the hallway, she slowed. "Now what?" They had time to kill and if she didn't stay busy the frustration was going to eat her alive.

A quick wicked grin flashed across Luca's face.

"I hear this place has a killer show and an amazing chef."

Annalise just shook her head. "You want to watch some showgirls shake their tail feathers?"

"No, I want to watch you shake your tail feathers, but since I doubt you'd be willing to get up on a stage in front of hundreds of people, I'll settle for the showgirls."

"You're incorrigible."

Luca shrugged. "Maybe, but I'm also a really fun date."

Is that what they were doing? Going on a date?

Annalise took a mental step back and tried to think. When was the last time she'd been on an honest-to-God date?

Months. Honestly, it might be closer to a year.

"I've got a better idea."

Luca's eyebrows shot up and his head tilted sideways. "I'm intrigued."

"I happen to have an in with one of the most exclusive clubs in the city. And I rarely cash in my sister chip."

"Then I think it's high time that you did."

Since they were dead in the water on the theft front, they'd both gone their separate ways for the rest of the day. Annalise still had a casino to run and there were a few loose ends that Luca needed to tie up on a business deal he'd been working the last several months.

But it had been difficult to let her go.

The bright side had been knowing he had another evening out with Annalise to look forward to when it was all said and done.

Since Excess was closer to the casino, Luca had volunteered to come back and pick her up. He'd taken the time to put on a nice suit—minus the tie; he never wore the things. He'd pulled his Maserati MC20 out of the garage. It was a pure toy, one he rarely took the time to enjoy.

Tonight felt like the perfect occasion to drive fast and play a little. Besides, he wanted to see the look on Annalise's face when he punched the pedal. Would she yell at him to slow down or laugh with excitement at the speed?

He honestly wasn't sure. A few weeks ago, he would have said she'd get irritated with him, but now... She had a hidden wild streak that very few got to see.

Pulling up to the front of the hotel, Luca had just tossed the keys to the valet and was about to head upstairs to Annalise's apartment when she came walking through the lobby doors.

Luca nearly swallowed his tongue when he saw her.

Her dress skimmed the top of her thighs, leaving the long expanse of her legs completely bare. The memory of pulling her panties off this morning in her office blasted through his mind.

Was it too much to hope that she was still naked under this skirt?

The dress was a combination of playful, sophisticated and siren all in one. The muted pale, dusty shade of blue played up the blond of her hair. The bodice was made entirely of lace, which teased him with glimpses of her skin beneath. The skirt flared out with just enough movement—and hope—that a stiff breeze might send the thing high enough for a glimpse of the promised land.

She'd paired the ensemble with nude strappy sandals that did wonderful things for her calves and thighs. Her hair was pulled up into an artfully messy knot on the top of her head. Luca wanted to tumble the whole thing down just to see the cloud of her gorgeous hair framing her face.

Of the handful of people milling about the entry to the hotel, almost all of them stopped and stared as Annalise walked through. Men, women, children, it didn't matter.

And she had no idea. She was oblivious to the attention. Her gaze was locked solely on him.

Pride, and something that resembled hope, swelled deep in his chest.

Tonight, she was his.

She glided up beside him, leaning forward to brush her lips across his cheek. Automatically, Luca wrapped an arm around her waist and pulled her tight against his body. His own lips found her ear and murmured, "You're beautiful every single day, but tonight you're absolutely stunning. Not because of the dress or the makeup or the shoes. But because you're glowing with a radiance that's all you."

Annalise let out a tiny, breathy sigh as her body melted against his.

"You're pretty handsome yourself, tiger." Pushing away, she took the opportunity to reach down and pinch his ass before tossing him a cheeky grin. "Let's go have some fun."

Sweeping her to the car, he waited until she'd settled into the seat before closing the door. The drive was a mixture of elation and discovery, even if it wasn't very long.

Annalise let her body settle back into the leather seat and didn't even reach for something to hold on to when he opened up the car and let it eat.

"Nice toy," she said, glancing over at him. But the grin playing around the corners of her mouth gave her away.

"Admit it. You like it."

With a laugh, she twisted to look at him. "Maybe."

It was clear, when they arrived at Excess, that Annalise had been truthful. She didn't often visit. The bouncer's wide eyes when he saw her and said hello gave her away. The man swept them inside, pausing to murmur something into the hidden earpiece.

It wasn't the first time Luca had visited Excess, although it wasn't like he played there every weekend. The atmosphere was expensive, sophisticated, exclusive and fun. The music was loud and current. The drinks were top-notch, and the food was gourmet. The who's who of Vegas and LA rubbed elbows with each other and the masses here.

Flashing lights, loud music, big crowds... They weren't what Luca generally craved. But tonight, he'd do anything to see the fire and laughter in Annalise's eyes.

Grasping his hand, Annalise leaned close and yelled "Follow me" over the pounding bass of some song he didn't recognize. Together, they snaked through tables and gyrating bodies to a set of stairs that led up to a balcony.

Another member of security stood on the landing but didn't stop them. Or anyone else.

Up above, there was more air. An array of couches, love seats and overstuffed chairs covered in jewel-toned velvet was scattered through the space. A bar at the far end supplied those who wanted a little less chaos with plenty of drink options.

People congregated in clusters and leaned against the clear plexiglass and metal railing that circled the balcony.

Annalise moved with purpose as she headed for the far corner. "Meredith prefers to stay above the melee," she threw over her shoulder, nodding to a knot tucked just beside the bar.

As they approached, Meredith leaped from the sofa, her dark red hair pulled back into a tight tail, and let out a squeal. Bounding over people, and dodging several small tables, she wrapped her arms around Annalise and pulled her in tight.

"Hell must be freezing over," she said, pushing away. "It's a random weeknight and you're at Excess? What the hell have you done with my best friend?"

Annalise grimaced. "I've been here before during the week."

"Sure, to yell at your brother or to talk about some

business thing. You've definitely never come out during the week dressed like that." Meredith held her friend at arm's length and let her gaze sweep down Annalise's body.

Luca completely understood the urge. He'd done it himself on more than one occasion since she'd walked out of the casino.

"Woman, you are fire. Where have you been hiding this dress?"

Looking down, Annalise flicked her hand in a dismissive gesture. "I've had this thing forever."

Rolling her eyes, Meredith grasped Annalise's arm and pulled her best friend behind her. Raising her voice, she said, "Michelle, can you take care of Lise?"

The bartender didn't even glance up, but responded, "On it."

Luca followed behind the pair, slightly bemused at the interaction.

He knew a little about Meredith Forrester because the stories she reported tended to make national headlines. The woman was a firecracker and full of energy. Looking at Annalise, he realized she was the cool and calm to her best friend's fire.

The pair settled on a sofa. Luca took the matching chair beside them.

Leaning forward, Meredith acknowledged him for the first time. "You'll have to tell me your secret. I've been trying to get her to come to Excess for months. She works too hard."

He wouldn't disagree with that statement. But before Luca could respond, Dominic slipped through a door that Luca hadn't even noticed hidden in the wall directly beside the bar and leaned over her from behind.

Meredith tipped her head backward and rose up to meet his kiss.

Her entire body glowed as she smiled up at him. "It's a family trait," she finally said, glancing back his way.

"So I've gathered."

Dominic reached into the space between them, offering his hand. "Good to see you, man. How are things going?"

His gaze swept between him and Annalise, splitting the question for the both of them. Luca understood exactly what the man was asking and waited for Annalise to respond. Her business, her issue, her lead.

"We're playing a waiting game at the moment. Running a couple programs that will take a while and hoping some new facial flags we've put in place will hit."

Dominic nodded. "Anything I can help with?"

Annalise's mouth twisted and her button nose wrinkled. "Not right now, but I'll let you know if that changes. I needed a distraction tonight."

Dominic's own mouth curled up into a knowing grin. He sent Luca a shared look. "The waiting game is killer, huh?"

"Nailed it in one."

"Well, you've come to the right place, then. Enjoy yourselves tonight." Dominic shifted, leaning forward so he could place a kiss on Annalise's forehead. "Work will be waiting in the morning."

Dominic set a hand on Meredith's shoulder and squeezed. "Speaking of which, there's an issue in Rio that I need to take care of."

Reaching up, Meredith set her own hand on top of his. Looking up, she said, "Don't forget to take your own advice."

"There are plenty of hours left in the night to enjoy," Dominic said, giving her a wicked grin that left little doubt as to exactly how he intended to enjoy those hours. With her.

Uncaring who was watching, Dominic wrapped a hand around the back of her neck and brought Meredith up for a deep kiss. It lasted seconds, but the expression on Meredith's face when he let her go was…enviable.

Her eyes were glassy and it seemed that in that moment Dominic Mercado was everything in her world.

Watching the two of them was…enlightening. And a little intimidating. Clearly, they loved each other, which was something Luca didn't quite understand. Oh, not the fact that you could care about another human being. That he got. There had been people in his life who had mattered over the years.

But it wasn't like he had a perfect example of what

a healthy relationship should be. He had no real reference for love, not even from his parents. They'd died when he was so young, he barely remembered them. He had a single photograph of them together when they were in their twenties. They looked happy... but nothing like the incandescent joy Meredith and Dominic shared.

If he was being honest, love wasn't something he'd ever spent much time contemplating. It wasn't a factor in his life, and until this moment, he'd never really missed it.

For some strange reason, his gaze traveled across to Annalise. Where he found her watching him, her head tipped sideways, a bemused expression on her face.

Eleven

Annalise had gotten used to Dominic and Meredith's public displays of affection. In fact, she'd sort of become jealous of them. They honestly didn't care who saw or knew that they were gaga for each other.

Which was sweet and sickening all at the same time. Especially when her brother was involved.

But watching Luca's reaction to them had been... unexpected.

At first, he'd been slightly taken aback. And then intrigued and puzzled. And finally, as envious as she sometimes was.

They'd stayed and talked with Meredith for a little while, catching up on the latest story she was researching.

Eventually, Luca took Annalise's hand and led her back downstairs to the main dance floor. She'd indulged in a couple drinks, not enough to make her buzzed, but enough to take the edge off any inhibitions she might have been harboring.

Spinning her out and back in, Luca let her body collide with his. He wrapped his arm around her waist. Tiny bubbles of happiness effervesced through her chest. Annalise leaned into his hold, throwing her head back and laughing. Despite everything, she was enjoying this night. Something she hadn't thought would be possible, all things considered.

They danced. Fast, slow, wild, until her body ached and sweat slicked her heated skin. She had no idea how long they were out on the floor. All Annalise knew was that each time Luca's hands touched her body, or his chest brushed against her breasts, the storm of need raging inside her ballooned and grew.

She wanted him. Not later. Not when they got back to the Magnifique. Now.

Luckily, because her brother owned Excess, she knew lots of private nooks and crannies.

The next time Luca's hand touched her body, Annalise wrapped her own fingers around his wrist and tugged.

His eyebrows winged up in silent question, but he followed as she started backing through the crowd. Her hips moved in time with the music, swaying seductively. The throb at the center of her sex pulsed in time with the staccato beat. Each step was torture as the lace of her panties rubbed against the slippery evidence of her desire.

There were two long hallways on either side of the main bar. The bathrooms were located down each, separated on purpose to cut down on the number of drunken men who "accidentally" stumbled into the women's restroom. Or, frankly, vice versa.

What most people didn't realize, by design, was that at the end of both was a doorway hidden in the far panel of the wall. Just like the one Dominic had used earlier. It was utilized mostly by staff to access both the executive offices and the storage areas and kitchen. There was another doorway behind the bar, which was used more often than these.

It wasn't until recently that Annalise had learned they were also used to protect women who were victims of domestic violence by secreting them away from their abusers without anyone knowing. Her brother, along with the help of Stone Surveillance, provided them with new identities and helped them start their lives over in safety.

Tonight, one hallway was going to be used for a much more pleasurable purpose.

As they passed the doorway to the restroom, Luca turned back around to gaze at it. The puzzled expression on his face was adorable. And sexy. It wasn't often that he was at a loss, which made Annalise even more excited.

"Where are we going? There's nothing down here, Annalise."

She ignored him, sliding her hand along the wall until she felt the latch and pushed. The door swung open with a soft click and gush of cool air. Soft, golden light tumbled through the open space. Beyond, muted sounds of metal clanking against metal rang from the kitchen. But she'd purposely chosen the hallway farthest from all that hustle and bustle.

Annalise dropped Luca's hand. Slipping through the open door, she gave him a come-hither gesture.

A grin played at the corners of his lips as he shook his head, but he followed anyway.

Once they were through, Annalise closed the door. From this side, it looked like any normal door. At the end of the new hallway a set of stairs led up to the Excess Inc. executive offices. No doubt, that's where Dominic would be. Luckily, there was another entrance from the offices down to the balcony where Meredith was, meaning there shouldn't be anyone up there interested in coming down this way.

In the midst of the crowded club, this tiny space was an oasis of privacy. One Annalise had every intention of taking advantage of.

"What are you up to, hmm?" The question buzzed through the back of Luca's throat.

"Making you pay for teasing me?"

One eyebrow rose. "How, exactly, was I teasing you?"

Annalise grinned at him. "Putting your hands on my waist." Grasping his hands, she placed them on her hips. "Brushing your hard chest against my breasts." Annalise moved closer, rubbing her own body against his. "Cupping my ass—" she slid one hand down to her rear "—and pulling me in tight so I could feel the hard ridge of your erection."

Luca's eyes sharpened with intensity, a swirl of passion and need that reverberated deep inside of her. "If I was teasing, so were you."

Raising an eyebrow of her own, she said, "The question is, what are you going to do about it?"

With a growl, Luca picked her up by the waist. He cupped her rear with both hands as she wrapped her legs and arms around him. He moved, each step rubbing her cloth-covered, swollen sex against the unforgiving ridge of his zipper. Her back hit the wall, but Annalise didn't care. A thud echoed through the quiet space, although no one was around to hear it except them.

Reaching between them, Luca hooked his fingers around the edge of her panties and pulled until the damp fabric tore.

"My panties are a real problem for you today, aren't they?"

"It would appear so."

Annalise probably would have made some off-hand quip, but every single thought flew out of her head when his fingers found the hot center of her sex and delved inside. The feel of his fingers had her crying out, thrusting up and searching for more.

He teased her. Rubbing his thumb over her clit as his fingers pumped faster and faster, in and out.

Her own breath sped up, matching his pace and the headlong rush toward an orgasm that flirted just around the edges of her senses.

"Oh, no, you don't," Luca rumbled, pulling his hand away.

The hidden muscles deep inside her body fluttered, oh so close to the orgasm she desperately needed. Annalise let out a garbled protest. It made sense in her head, although the words came out all wrong. Apparently, Luca understood her anyway.

"Trust me, princess," he murmured even as his hand fumbled with the fly on his pants.

The strange thing was that she did.

Impatient, Annalise brushed him away. She jerked the zipper down and yanked the button so hard it popped off his pants, pinging onto the floor and rolling away.

Annalise reached inside, finding the long, hard, hot length of him with her fist. His skin was velvet over steel as she stroked, up and down, relishing the feel of him against her palm. A tiny pearl of moisture collected at the tip and she couldn't stop herself from swiping across it with her thumb.

Luca was the one to groan this time.

Positioning the head of his cock at the entrance to her sex, Annalise urged him on. "Hurry. Please."

The feel of him as he thrust home was pure bliss. Everything else faded away. A storm built, the two of them centered directly at the apex, feeding off each other. Luca thrust, in and out, faster and faster, even as she grasped his ass and used her clenched fingers to demand more.

She needed more. Everything he could give her.

The orgasm slammed into her, sudden and breath-stealing. Every muscle in her body locked as ecstasy pounded through her. She was aware enough to register Luca's own release as he joined her. The rhythmic pulse and his gut-deep groan of relief.

His forehead dropped to the crook of her shoulder. Labored puffs of breath rushed against her skin. And held tight against his chest, she could feel the energetic stampede of his heart.

Annalise had no idea how long they stood there, her back pinned against the wall from the weight of his body. Not that she cared. Slowly, her senses came back online. Delicious scents floated on the circulating air from the kitchen. The thump of music reverberated through the wall at her back.

Slowly, they disengaged. Luca helped her right her clothes as he did the same. They were quiet, and for a moment, Annalise struggled with a blast of uncertainty.

But that disappeared when Luca reached for her, pulled her close and touched his mouth to hers.

The kiss wasn't about rekindling the energy they'd just blown. It wasn't about seduction or sex. It was about something deeper. A connection she'd never felt with anyone else.

A lump formed in the back of her throat.

Crap, she was in trouble.

Fear and uneasiness twisted in her gut. She might have said something—probably something stupid—but the sound of metal clanging from the other end of the hallway had her startling and jumping away.

"The door," she mock whispered.

Someone was coming. And suddenly she felt like a teenager caught necking in the woods. Thank God whoever was headed their way hadn't shown up five minutes ago.

"There you are. Meredith was worried." Dominic strode toward them down the hallway, his pointed gaze sharp as a tack.

If Luca had a thinner skin, the other man's obvious censure might have bothered him. But it didn't. Luca really didn't care what Annalise's brother thought of him.

No, that wasn't entirely true. But he also didn't care if the man had a problem with what he and Annalise had just shared. Because even though the other man might not have caught them in the middle of the act, it was pretty obvious they'd been engaged in sex.

Annalise's hair tumbled around her face, clearly disheveled. Her lips were pink and swollen and her skin was flushed with the heat of a good orgasm.

Trying to cover for them, Annalise cleared her throat. "I was just showing Luca up to the executive offices. And looking for you."

Dominic's eyebrows winged up. "Uh-huh." Clearly, he didn't believe her excuse.

"We're going to head out and I wanted to tell you goodbye."

"We are?" That was news to Luca. He'd been enjoying the night with Annalise, seeing her carefree and indulging herself.

He was about to argue that he could go all night if she wanted to stay longer, but the trilling tone from his phone stopped him.

Reaching into his pocket, Luca pulled it out to glance at the screen. Throwing them an apologetic look, he said, "I have to take this," and excused himself down the hallway.

Behind him, he could hear Annalise and Dominic as they murmured to each other. He didn't have to be a genius to figure out by the tone that Dominic was busy pulling out the big brother card while Annalise was playing the grown adult counter.

Luca didn't bother with pleasantries, but answered the call with "What have you got?" There was only one reason Joker would be calling this late—or early, depending on how you looked at it.

"It isn't good, man."

Luca let out a silent groan. Joker was excellent at uncovering information. Luca didn't ask pointed questions and it was better for everyone involved that that was the case. However, he rarely got emotional or cared about what he discovered. Like that old TV show, Joker's mantra was "just the facts." Information was black-and-white. People made it gray or red or even purple. Joker passed on info, usually nothing more. If he ever had opinions, he'd always kept them to himself.

But not this time. Clearly, the other man was not happy with whatever he'd learned. Luca could hear the regret in his voice. This wasn't going to be good.

"Tell me."

Luca listened as Joker laid out the details of what he'd learned, a pit building bigger and bigger in his belly with each word. Annalise was going to be devastated and he was the one about to crumble her foundation.

Goddammit.

Luca listened quietly, asking a few pointed questions before ending the call with "Thanks, man. I appreciate it. I'll talk with Annalise and let you know if I need anything else."

Hanging up the phone, he stood there for several seconds, staring at the plain gray wall across from him. He held the phone so tightly that the edges of it pinched the palm of his hand. Turning slowly, he took in the sight of Annalise and Dominic at the end of the hall.

They stood, close together, their heads bent toward each other. It was clear from their expressions that they were irritated with each other. But it was also evident from their body language that they cared.

He watched the brother and sister, the visual evidence of their connection screaming at him.

He'd never experienced that kind of closeness.

With anyone. He'd never had someone who would pull him aside and tell him a hard truth because they cared about him and wanted to help him avoid a costly mistake.

He'd learned all of his lessons the hard way.

As if sensing his study, Annalise glanced his way. "Everything okay?"

Luca nodded even as he said, "We do need to head back, actually."

In a split second, Annalise was at his side, her questioning gaze searching his face.

Shaking his head, he said, "In the car."

Her mouth thinned, but she didn't push. Instead, she turned to Dominic. "Apologize to Meredith that I left without saying goodbye. I'll give her a call tomorrow."

Dominic nodded. "Let me know if there's anything I can do." It was a little disconcerting when his gaze swept across Luca, including him in the offer.

They used another hallway through the kitchen to exit to the side of the building. The sparkle of the evening had been shattered, and not even slipping into the soft leather seats of his MC20 could revive it.

Annalise had barely clicked her seat belt before turning to him. "Spill it."

With a sigh, Luca forced himself to focus on the road and calmly shared what Joker had discovered.

"I asked Joker to look into the list of names we pulled."

"You did what?" The way Annalise's voice tipped

up at the end left little doubt that she was upset. He'd known she would be, which was why he hadn't mentioned it.

If Joker found nothing, no harm, no foul. If he found something it would be hard to argue that his methods hadn't produced results.

"I told you I didn't want someone digging into the backgrounds of people who worked for my company."

Luca's hands tightened on the steering wheel, his knuckles going white. "Yes, you did. But only one of those names was a former employee. Someone who doesn't work for the Magnifique anymore."

"You're splitting hairs."

Maybe he was.

Annalise's words rushed into the small space between them, filling it up and making the knots in his belly tighten. "You knew how I'd feel, but you did it anyway." She didn't bother making it a question because obviously that was exactly what he'd done.

"It was the right thing to do, Annalise. I knew it would be a decision you didn't feel comfortable making, so I made it for you."

Golden light flashed through her eyes, straight-up irritation and anger. "I didn't ask you to do that."

"Nevertheless. I did it. And what Joker found is important."

Annalise crossed her arms over her chest and turned her body toward the door. Her gaze jerked to the passenger window. Her face was drawn and closed, completely different from the open, carefree woman he'd been dancing with not an hour before.

He let her process, knowing she needed time to come to some sort of acceptance.

"I don't appreciate you going behind my back," she finally said.

"I understand and don't blame you." He didn't. He understood, but also recognized that she wouldn't have agreed to the search, even though it was the smart thing to do.

"But you're not sorry you did it." Again, not a question because she already knew the answer.

Honestly, he wasn't, even if he didn't like the way her body suddenly screamed "closed off." "No. I'd do it again."

Reaching up, Annalise rubbed her fingers against her forehead. "Do you understand how frustrating that is? You knew what my response would be, it didn't matter to you, you didn't agree, so you ignored my wishes."

A blinding realization slammed through Luca.

Annalise didn't trust him, and probably never would. She'd always see him as the cheater her father had beaten and thrown into the street like so much trash. No matter what he did, no matter how many times he tried to protect her, help her or support her, she wouldn't see things from that perspective.

She'd always assume his intentions were false and tinged with self-interest.

There was no winning, but for some reason, he felt the need to try.

"No, I didn't ignore your wishes. I recognized that your overblown sense of loyalty—a sense of loyalty others around you don't feel and haven't necessarily earned—would prevent you from seeing that this was the right move to take. I was protecting you from yourself, Annalise."

Her loud sigh echoed through the car. "This conversation is pointless because nothing will change. You're certain you were right, and I'm certain you were wrong. What did Joker learn?"

A sharp pain lanced through Luca's chest. It was unfamiliar, unpleasant and hurt like a son of a bitch.

He couldn't do anything about that unwelcome sensation right now. But he could focus on the thief.

"Did you know Robert had a sister?"

"Yes, she's much younger than he is. Like fifteen or sixteen years younger."

Luca shook his head. He really didn't want to be the one to deliver this news. "Was."

"What?"

Luca glanced her way, pausing for the briefest moment to appreciate the way the moonlight gilded her hair. "You said *is*. It should be *was*. She committed suicide about a year and a half ago."

"I had no idea."

It was Luca's turn to sigh. "I figured as much. She had a gambling problem. A big one. She'd been in treatment off and on for almost six years, but apparently that last downhill slide was bad."

Annalise's eyebrows pulled together in a deep frown. "If I'd known, I would have done something."

He also knew that was true. Even though Robert had already retired from the Magnifique when it happened, if Annalise had been aware, she would have offered help.

"She had a lot of debt. To some nasty people. I gather Robert got involved. Or the nasty people dragged him into it. Either way, Emily, his sister, decided the best way out was to just remove herself from the equation."

Annalise closed her eyes, screwing them shut for several seconds. "That's not how those people work."

"No, it isn't. They came after Robert. Put him in the hospital for a day with a broken ankle. He withdrew everything he had from his retirement. It wasn't enough."

"So you think he started stealing from the Magnifique to get the rest?"

Luca shrugged. "I don't know. I can tell you he's still alive, so he must have worked out something with the circling sharks."

Annalise's head dropped back against the headrest. Her entire body sagged, with exhaustion and defeat. Luca hated to see her this way and hated to be the source of her pain. "Assuming this is all true."

"It is." Of that, he was certain.

"It isn't exactly a smoking gun."

No, he didn't suppose it was. Although, in his mind it was clearly a motive. The man needed money and if his position with the Magnifique had given him a way to get access to easy cash...

"I understand your point. Based on the patterns we've been seeing, the thief is due for another run. I suggest we sit and wait. The names have already been flagged, including Robert's. Now, it's just a matter of time."

Twelve

It had been a nerve-wracking few days. Almost like she was constantly waiting for the other shoe to drop. Her shoulders were knotted and she hadn't been sleeping well.

Luca had been spending most of his time working on a project of his own, away from the Magnifique, which wasn't helping much. He'd seemed distant and preoccupied, but when she'd asked him what was going on he'd simply explained that his own project had hit a bump that needed his attention.

There wasn't much for them to do on the thief front, anyway.

But it was difficult not to take his pulling away personally. Although, it was just one more reminder of why she couldn't let herself get attached. Whatever they were doing…it was amazing, but it wasn't permanent.

Luca always walked away. That was what she needed to remember.

But when they were together, remembering was difficult.

Despite her irritation with what he'd done, she still wanted him. No, if she was being honest with herself, she needed him.

One evening he'd invited her over to his place, where he'd made her a delicious dinner and they'd spent the rest of the night in his huge bed. Somehow, even doing the most mundane and domestic things, he made her feel special. It was the way he looked at her, those gray eyes intense and hungry. Like he was dying of thirst and she was the only one who could slake it.

He'd shown her his home. They'd eaten on the back patio surrounded by the soft sound of water lapping at the edge of the pool and the stars above for a romantic backdrop. Wine, candles and muted music. A gentle breeze had even kept the worst of the heat at bay.

And in the morning, he'd made her waffles with strawberries and whipped cream.

The experience had felt like the scene from a movie, almost too perfect.

And then she hadn't seen him for two days.

When they were together, it was amazing. When

they were apart, Annalise couldn't help the doubts that crept in and consumed her thoughts. Luca confused her. But it didn't matter, because he also intrigued her.

She wanted to be the kind of woman to say screw him for disappearing. Again. And with any other man, she wouldn't have a problem doing it. She'd had her fair share of walking away.

Why couldn't she be that way with him?

No, she had to dream about the man, waking aching and burning with desire. She had to fight a tiny spurt of disappointment each time the phone rang and it wasn't him. And she hated herself just a tiny bit because she couldn't control her response.

Tension had been building, and it wasn't only affecting her. Annalise realized that her own staff were picking up on her unintentional signals and had started approaching her with caution. Like she was a grumpy bear about to snap their heads off.

Not good.

For the second time in twenty minutes, Annalise realized she'd been staring at the report on her computer screen without really seeing the numbers. Apparently, she needed a break. And she was just about to shut her computer down and call it a night when Luca walked into her office.

First, happiness bubbled through her chest. Followed quickly by irritation.

"You're still working?" he asked, plopping down in the chair across from her. One ankle crossed over a knee, he sprawled backward, lazily running his gaze across her face.

"Yes, I'm still working." Annalise had no idea the irritation was going to come out in her words until they were in the air. Too late to call them back. She needed to get a grip before he realized what was going on in her head.

They weren't exactly in a place where she could be possessive of his time, or jealous that he hadn't been spending all of it with her. Or any of it as the case may be.

"Why don't we head up for a quick update with security and then enjoy one of the restaurants downstairs?"

Suddenly, Annalise's stomach grumbled. He probably couldn't hear it, but she definitely felt it. And she realized she hadn't bothered to eat anything since the protein bar she'd mindlessly munched around nine this morning.

Part of her wanted to be snarly and make a point. The rest of her just wanted to enjoy spending time with him while she could. And that side won out.

"That sounds like a wonderful plan."

Tapping a few keys, Annalise closed the report and shut down her system. Grabbing her key card, she rose from her desk and crossed to pass him for the door.

But she didn't make it very far.

Reaching out, he snagged her hand and, before she realized what he was planning, had her tumbled into his lap.

She sprawled, haphazardly and inelegantly, across his spread thighs. But Luca didn't seem to notice or care. His palm cupped the back of her neck and his mouth found hers in a drugging kiss.

Everything else faded from existence except the way he made her feel. Her irritation whispered away as if it had been made of smoke. And she was left with nothing but the burning fire he stoked deep inside.

"I've missed you," he murmured against her mouth. "I'm sorry I haven't been here the past couple days."

Annalise started to make some flippant quip about not even noticing but stopped herself. It wasn't true, and something urged her to be honest with him.

"I missed you too. More than I'd like to admit."

A smile tugged at Luca's lips and his eyes flashed with a muted sense of humor. "That I totally understand. I'm not used to being so…interested in someone else, Annalise. It makes me uneasy sometimes. But not enough to walk away."

Yet.

He might not have said the word, but Annalise heard it nonetheless.

Pulling away was an exercise in self-preservation as she struggled to regain her feet.

"Let's go check upstairs. I'm starving."

Luca walked into the security hub. The bank of glowing monitors and the handful of people staring at them was familiar territory.

The hustle of activity they'd walked into seemed… unusual. While most people might think security work was interesting and high energy, those moments were actually few and far between. Most of it was boring and tedious. Staring at video or combing through information hoping to find the one piece that didn't fit.

Clearly, they'd stumbled into the middle of something.

Annalise, probably unaware of what the increased activity could mean, made her way through the controlled chaos and into the office at the far end. Nick sat behind the desk, staring at a screen of his own, a frown pulling his already drooping jowls even lower.

He glanced up, a preoccupied expression on his face. "Annalise, I was just about to call you."

"Oh?"

With a sigh, Nick leaned back in his chair. "One of the cards we flagged popped up in the system."

"Great. Which one?"

He glanced at the screen in front of him. "Connie Marksman, although the facial recognition software didn't alert us to her entering the casino. We're in the process of trying to figure out why."

Luca stepped up beside Annalise, pressing his palms to the edge of the desk and leaning slightly forward. "Is Connie playing at a slot machine?"

"She was, but by the time the system pinged she'd already left the machine. With a win."

Of course she had. "Pull up the footage from that

machine for the last half hour." Rounding the desk, Luca stood behind the other man as Nick did what he'd asked.

Annalise joined them. The tantalizing scent of her teased Luca's senses. Her hand landed on the flat of his waist as she steadied herself against him for a better look at the screen.

Together, they all watched, glued to the monitor as Nick scrolled through the footage.

"That's the machine," he said, pointing at one to the far right in a row at the bottom of the screen.

The angle of the camera showed the back of the person sitting there, but not much else. Faces were caught as people either sat or exited from in front of the machine. Whoever it was wore a long coat that hid their body and a ball cap.

Hitting a button, the people on-screen began to fast-forward through their motions.

All three of them watched, eyes tracking as people entered and exited the frame. None of them spoke. Hell, they barely breathed.

Until Annalise let out a startled gasp.

Luca didn't understand, but he didn't really have to. This wasn't going to be good.

A man walked through the frame, looking around him. He sat at the machine they were watching, and Nick hit another button to pause the recording. Glancing back, he sent an apologetic expression Annalise's way.

"That's Connie."

Swallowing, Annalise shook her head, saying exactly what Luca had feared. "No, that's Robert."

A pit dropped through his stomach. He'd really been hoping he was wrong. But it was actually worse than he'd feared.

His initial thought was that Robert might have shared information in exchange for forgiveness of his sister's debt. And that a handful of people were using the doctored reward cards to insert malware and force the machines to pay out at specific times.

But clearly, if he was using Connie Marksman's card, then he was behind all of the thefts. They didn't have a ring of thieves. They had a single thief.

And it was someone Annalise knew, trusted and counted as family.

"Why didn't the facial rec ping when he entered?" Annalise asked.

Nick cut his eyes up and to the left. "It did, but I assumed it was a mistake. This is Robert we're talking about. Why didn't you tell me he was a suspect?"

Now wasn't the time to talk about it. They needed to find Robert before he slipped back through their fingers. When the man on tape stood up from the machine, Luca ordered, "Follow him with the cameras."

Even as they continued to watch the feed, switching to different cameras' footage as needed, several staff members, oblivious to what was going on, approached Robert. They gave him hugs and smiles as they spoke. Glancing over, Luca took in Annalise's expression. Devastation. Disappointment. Anger. Hope.

"Maybe there's a perfectly logical explanation."

Her gaze swung to his and everything she was feeling pounded into him.

He hated to be the person to burst the perfect ideal that she'd built around her existence. After hearing the story of what she'd experienced as a child, he understood her need to build a family that she could trust. Something she'd done with her employees. She could be the mother figure, solving all their problems and all she asked for in return was loyalty and a sense of safety.

But that wasn't how the world really worked. And he, better than most, understood that.

It still hurt to bring that world crashing down on her head.

"There isn't. And you know it." He tried to make the words gentle, but somehow, they still sounded harsh to him.

Shaking her head, Annalise tried to deny what she knew was right.

"Ma'am?" Nick called to them.

They both returned their gaze to the screens. "We found him on the live feed. He just sat down at another machine."

"What card did he use?"

Nick's mouth thinned into a tight line. "Daniel Salcedo."

As far as Luca was concerned, that was irrefutable proof they'd caught their thief. But he wasn't the person in charge.

It took everything he had not to issue the order to grab him. That wasn't his call.

Luca waited, for some reason a knot of fear and disappointment tight in his belly.

Until Annalise said, "Send someone to get him. Tell him I'd like to speak with him. Hopefully, he'll follow quietly. Bring him to the holding room."

Annalise spun on her heels, striding through the room and out into the hallway. Luca followed, even though she hadn't indicated she wanted him to.

He found her, back against the wall, spine curved and her head in her hands. At first, he thought she might have been crying, but when he reached her, she dropped her hands away and looked up at him.

Her eyes burned with anger. Her entire face was flushed with it. In that moment, he recognized that she was indeed her father's daughter.

He'd once been on the receiving end of a look almost identical…right before her father had two men beat the crap out of him.

"What are you doing to do?"

"I'm going to gather the evidence we have so far, including the time-stamped video and matching card data and turn it over to the police."

"I know this is hard for you, Annalise."

She grimaced. "Life is hard. I learned that lesson a long time ago, Luca."

The grim determination in her voice scared him. Gone was the competent, cool and focused woman he'd gotten to know over the past few weeks.

At the moment, she was a bundle of emotions, none of them good. Oh, she was holding them in, but he could see the evidence, bubbling just beneath the surface.

Which was almost more dangerous. At some point, those emotions were going to get the better of her. She couldn't hold them in forever and that explosion wouldn't be good for anyone, especially her.

"Maybe you should call in Dominic to help you deal with this." Her brother might function as the cooler head in this situation. He didn't have emotional ties to the man who had just betrayed Annalise.

Her roiling gaze sharpened. "Why would I do that? I can handle this just fine, Luca. Without help from anyone."

One of the security staff poked his head out the door. "Ma'am, he's waiting for you."

Annalise acknowledged the message with a nod and turned her back on him. Punching up the elevator, he slipped into the car beside her. They were both silent as it dropped them slowly to the basement.

They exited at the ding into an environment completely foreign from the one they'd just left. Gone was the elegance and opulence of the casino floor. Or the coolly professional decor of the offices. Exposed cinder block and stark, institutional lights surrounded them. Everything about the place screamed functional and nothing more.

Memories slammed into him and the ache in his hip throbbed with renewed effort. It rarely bothered him, but moments like these, when something sent him flashing back in time, his mind liked to play tricks.

He could practically feel the pinch of tight fingers around his arm as one of the security staff marched him down this same hallway. Another followed closely behind in case Luca decided to try something stupid.

He remembered the harsh fluorescent light as it stung his eyes and the cocky way he'd taunted the silent men as they moved him where they wanted.

He'd been young, stupid and confident that they really couldn't do much to him. Card counting might be frowned on by the casinos, but it wasn't illegal. They couldn't have him arrested. They could throw him out and blackball him, but that was it. And while he'd miss the opportunity to stretch his brain and make a quick buck to cover the exorbitant cost of college tuition, there were other options out there for him.

And casinos off the beaten path that probably wouldn't get the memo from the Magnifique. He'd find other games and other ways.

That cockiness had powered his mouth when Mac Mercado had walked into the tiny sterile room.

Already angry, it hadn't taken long for the two to clash. And for fists to start pounding. In that moment, Luca realized the error of his assumption. There was something they could do to him. Something that hurt. A lot.

Luca had no idea if the doorway they stopped in front of now was the same one he'd gone through.

It looked familiar, but all the doors in the hallway looked the same.

Not that it particularly mattered.

Annalise paused and he took the opportunity to grasp her arm and pull her around to face him.

The anger he'd seen before still rushed beneath the surface of her expression. No doubt, she was using it to hold the hurt at bay. But he didn't want to see her use it to make a decision that she'd later regret.

"Promise me that when we walk in there, you won't do something stupid."

She tilted her head sideways. "Stupid?"

His own mouth thinned. "Look, I've been the guy sitting behind that table. Don't do something you'll regret."

Shock slacked her features for a brief moment before anger sharpened them again.

"Do you really think I'm going to have him beaten? You've met most of my security staff. Do you think they're the kind of men and women capable of following that type of order even if I gave it?"

Luca frowned. "Most of your staff would do anything for you, Annalise."

Her honey eyes sharpened even more. "You know my childhood. I witnessed abuse on more than one occasion. I watched as my mother was murdered. And you think I'm capable of walking through that door not just to witness more, but to instigate it?"

Her teeth clacked together as her jaw snapped shut. But it didn't stay that way for long. "I despise what my father did to you. I've struggled with that experience for years. He's my dad, and frankly the only safe haven I had as a child. I grew up thinking he was larger than life and could do no wrong. Until that day. You had your leg shattered and bruises all across your body. I don't dismiss the trauma done to you. But I had my entire world ripped out from under me. For the second time. And the fact that you think I could be capable of inflicting that pain on anyone else, especially someone I've counted as a friend for years…"

She shook her head. "I don't have time for this. I appreciate everything you've done to help here. Go home, your job is done. You're no longer wanted."

The words pierced Luca's chest just as surely as any bullet might have.

She'd more than dismissed him. She'd crushed any fledgling idea that they could have more. Be more.

But why was he surprised? Why would Annalise be any different from anyone else?

No one had ever wanted him.

And he'd built a life making sure that he didn't need anyone either. For a few weeks, he'd forgotten that fact.

She'd done him a favor by reminding him.

Thirteen

Annalise walked through the door and every emotion she'd been fighting crashed over her. Hurt, disappointment, anger and pain.

But she didn't have time for those things. Not right now.

Gritting her teeth, Annalise steeled her body and willed it to keep moving. At least for a little while. After the details were taken care of, then she could collapse.

But not until then.

"Ms. Mercado," Robert said, standing partway up from his chair. One of her security staff, a man positioned against the far wall, took a step closer, stalling Robert's motion halfway up.

"Sit," she said, waving her hand. "There are a few things we need to talk about, Robert."

His body sank and the minute his bottom hit the chair an avalanche of emotion crossed his face. Fear, guilt, anger and finally determination.

"I know what this is about." Robert's voice trembled. Annalise wasn't sure if it was fear or guilt or some combination of the two. But it wouldn't sway her.

"Do you?"

He nodded. "I knew eventually I'd get caught."

No evasion. No attempt at denial. No explanation that she might be able to live with. That hurt almost as much as Robert's betrayal.

"Why did you do it? If you needed money that badly, Robert, why didn't you just come to me?"

His mouth twisted. "It isn't just about the money, Ms. Mercado."

"Then what is it about?"

"Casinos took everything from my sister. And then they took everything from me."

"No." Annalise shook her head. "Addiction took those things from you and your sister."

His face turned red and his sad eyes went watery with unshed tears. "That's exactly what people said to me when Emily died. *It's such a shame. Addiction is such a terrible disease.* And it is."

Robert balled his fists and hit the table, rattling the metal legs. Annalise fought hard not to jump, but the two security guards standing at the door started forward. She waved them still.

Robert wasn't even aware. His gaze bored into hers. "Why does she have to be the only one to take the brunt of the blame? Casinos make it possible and living in Vegas makes it impossible to avoid the casinos. Did you know she sought treatment four times before killing herself?"

The pain in Robert's voice echoed through her own chest. Annalise had been there, mourning the loss of someone very important and feeling helpless to seek justice for the tragedy of that loss.

"I'm sorry, Robert, but that doesn't make what you did okay."

"You don't think I know that?" Desperation tinged his words. "It started out as a way to pay the debt and protect my own family."

"But it turned into something more?" Annalise asked the question, but deep down, she already knew the answer.

"Yes." The single word blasted between them, full of accusation and justification. "I was angry. And then the money was nice. I took the family on a vacation, all the grandkids. I gave my son the down payment for his first house. And bought my daughter a new car."

She wondered why his children never questioned where the newfound wealth had come from, but at the end of the day, it didn't matter.

"I had the means to make the gambling industry pay, and I took it."

"Except you didn't make anyone pay except for

me. The Magnifique. The family you worked with for thirty years. Your friends and colleagues."

He shrugged. "I know, but I had the knowledge to use here and a back door that I'd installed almost seven years ago."

"You've been planning this for that long?"

"No, of course not. It started out as a way to ensure if someone hacked our system and took over that we could regain control. But when I realized I needed money…"

"You used it for your own purposes."

"Yes." Robert slumped back into the chair. His shoulders rounded and all the fight and fire just disappeared from his gaze. "What's going to happen now?"

Annalise stared at him. A huge part of her—the little girl who'd watched her mother die violently at the hands of someone she once trusted—wanted to drop the whole thing and tell him that nothing would happen.

And maybe, if he'd simply taken the funds he needed to cover the debt and protect his family, she might have been willing to do that. But it had gotten too big.

"The police have been contacted. I'll be turning over the evidence we've gathered. I'm certain they'll be pressing charges."

Robert nodded. "My wife will be devastated."

No doubt. "I'm sorry for that, Robert. But my hands are tied here."

"I understand."

Her heart heavy, Annalise pushed up from the table. She paused inside the open doorway, turning to glance at the man she'd considered her friend.

He looked dejected and small.

She couldn't look at him anymore.

Closing the door behind her, she paused to speak to one of the security team hovering in the hallway. "Let Nick know that I've gone back upstairs. I'd like a complete report before he leaves tonight."

"Yes, ma'am."

Taking the elevator, Annalise stopped at her office. Several people were still moving about, although in the next hour or so the offices would be completely empty for the night.

She'd half expected to see Luca waiting for her. But he wasn't there.

And neither were any of the things he'd randomly left in her office over the past few weeks. While she'd been speaking with Robert, he'd cleared out and left.

On top of everything else, the weight of his absence was just too much.

Tears stung the backs of her eyes, but Annalise refused to let them fall. She wasn't that kind of woman. Life had made her stronger than that.

Turning on her heel, she went up to her apartment. It wasn't like she would be able to concentrate on anything else tonight, anyway.

For the first time in her life, the penthouse felt cold and empty when she walked inside. The gorgeous view out the windows didn't calm or impress her as it usually did. Not even pouring a glass of wine and enjoying it on her balcony seemed worth the effort.

Instead, she sank onto her sofa and curled her feet beneath her.

A strangled sound broke from deep inside.

It hurt. Everything that had happened today hurt. Robert. Luca. Feeling betrayed by both.

She'd placed her trust and faith in two men who obviously hadn't deserved it.

Robert wasn't her fault. There had been no indication of a problem until it was too late.

But with Luca...she'd known better. Hell, her brother had all but warned her that Luca Kilpatrick didn't stick around for anything or anyone. Not even the projects he invested blood, sweat and years into. He created, he invented, he used his brilliant mind to solve problems, and then he walked away to let someone else handle the day-to-day drudgery.

Certainly, she'd told him he wasn't needed in the interrogation room, but that hadn't meant she expected him to clear his stuff and leave without another word. But hadn't she always known this is how things would end?

Luca didn't let anyone in. And, yes, she understood that stemmed from his own twisted childhood. But that didn't make the situation any easier to bear.

In fact, it made it harder. Because somewhere

deep inside, she'd let herself truly believe that maybe he could be different for her. With her.

But that wasn't how life worked.

Luca was who he was and he'd made no promises or indications otherwise. The pain she was feeling was her own doing.

She couldn't even be mad at him. No, that wasn't true. She was pretty mad. What she couldn't do was blame him.

What she *could* do was pick up the pieces and move on with her life. Enjoy the moments they'd shared for what they were and count herself lucky to have had the experience of knowing him, if only for a little while.

And that was exactly what she was going to do. Tomorrow.

It had been several days since they'd caught Robert.

Annalise had spent that time returning to the normal routine of running the casino. Until she no longer had the puzzle of the theft hanging over her head, she hadn't realized just how much of her attention and energy it had taken.

But that wasn't necessarily a good thing.

She'd spent the last few days vacillating between being short with her staff, angry at everyone and lonely in the evenings by herself. Tonight, she was determined not to sit at home again and was in the process of getting ready to head to Excess.

At least there she could see Meredith and Dominic.

The music was loud and the flashing lights hurt her eyes, but Annalise refused to leave. She had a couple drinks and forced herself to dance a little, although the memory of the last time she'd been there was like a knife to her chest.

Meredith glanced over at her as she collapsed onto the sofa in the upstairs balcony. "Everything okay?"

"Yeah," Annalise insisted, pasting a smile on her face that she didn't really feel.

Meredith's narrowed gaze studied her for several seconds, but she didn't push, which Annalise was eternally grateful for. She was holding everything in by sheer will and wasn't ready to share just yet. Not even with her best friend.

A guy approached the sofa, leaning close to speak over the roar of the music. "Would you like to dance?"

Annalise glanced at him. He wasn't anything special, but he also wasn't anything terrible. He was handsome and dressed well. Clearly successful, or at least with the ability to pretend that he was. He appeared polite.

But he wasn't Luca.

Which was exactly why she held out her hand and said yes.

She needed to let go of the fantasy she'd built in her head and tonight was as good a time as any.

They made their way back downstairs. The music was fast and it was easy to gyrate her body and let the beat of it seduce her into letting go. The guy, Marcus, was a good dancer. He had rhythm and a confidence that said he didn't care what anyone thought of him, as long as they were enjoying themselves. A couple times, she caught him laughing at himself.

Any other time she might have been charmed by his attempts at conversation and dance moves.

Everything was fine, until the music slowed and he reached for her.

The minute his hands touched her waist, she wanted out. Away.

Panic welled up deep inside her chest. Not because she was afraid that he'd hurt her—he'd given no indication that he would—but because she didn't want to be vulnerable.

Making a quick apology, she left him staring at her on the dance floor as she retreated.

Annalise's feet pounded up the steps to the balcony, but she didn't stop there. Charging for the hidden door, she slipped into the quiet safety of the hallway and headed for Dominic's executive suite.

She heard the door open and shut behind her, knew Meredith had followed, but she didn't slow down.

Her chest felt like someone had placed a two-ton weight on it. Suddenly, she couldn't breathe and the pleasant warmth of dancing turned into a raging fire beneath her skin. She wanted to rip off her clothes. Get relief.

But there was none.

Bursting into her brother's office, she collapsed

onto the cool surface of the oversize leather chair in the far corner. Her brother turned from his vantage point at the wall of windows overlooking the club. She knew he often stood up here and watched over his domain.

Meredith followed her into the office, quietly shutting the door.

Annalise leaned forward, dropped her face into her hands and tried desperately to pull enough air into her lungs.

The arm beside her creaked as Meredith sat beside her. The soft comfort of her hand rubbed down Annalise's back. "Just breathe."

Slowly, the panic eased. The weight on her chest lifted and suddenly she was bone-deep tired.

Squeezing her eyes shut, Annalise stayed there for a few more minutes than she needed. She wasn't ready to deal with the two silent sentries watching her emotional breakdown.

But she knew she wasn't getting out of this room without at least giving them some explanation as to what was going on. She might as well get it over with so that she could go home.

Coming to Excess tonight had been a bad idea.

Dropping her hands, Annalise shifted back into the chair and let the cushions take her weight.

"You want to tell us what's going on?" Meredith's voice was soft and easy. She didn't press. Annalise had heard that tone from her before, when she was interviewing emotional subjects for her stories. She had a way of making people feel comfortable and safe. That's why people trusted and confided in her.

"Not really."

On the far side of the room, Dominic stirred. "You're going to do it anyway, right?"

Annalise grimaced. Like her big brother was going to give her a real choice.

"This week has just been…difficult." And that was the understatement of the year.

"I knew Robert's betrayal would hurt. You considered him family," Meredith said. "But that's not everything, is it? Where's Luca?"

The tiny throb of pain returned to her chest. "I have no idea. He left the Magnifique while I was speaking with Robert. Took all his stuff with him. I haven't heard from him since."

Meredith sucked in a sharp breath. Thunder rolled across Dominic's already dark expression. "I'm going to kill him."

"You're going to do no such thing," Annalise said, although there was no heat or force behind her words. Part of her—the weakest part—liked the idea of her brother ripping into Luca for leaving her. The rest of her realized that she was perfectly capable of taking care of herself.

Besides, she had told him to leave… She just hadn't meant permanently. She'd needed space to deal with what was in front of her. He'd definitely given her space. But it was the reminder she needed that this was who Luca was. And the pain she was feeling was inevitable. Better to get it over with now so that she could move on with her life.

If she wanted to confront Luca, she would. But, really, what was there to say? They'd made no promises to each other. Hell, they'd barely even dated. They'd shared some heat. That was all.

"He hasn't done anything wrong. Leave him alone, Nic. I mean it."

Her brother's expression sharpened. He didn't agree, but he also didn't say that he would go after the other man no matter what. And knowing her brother, that was as close to a concession as she was going to get on this one.

"Honestly, I think it's the back-to-back betrayals that have rocked my world. I've been hell to work with the last few days. Instead of being happy that we finally caught the thief and solved the problem, everyone is walking on eggshells, afraid to say anything. I've lost my temper more than once."

"Which isn't like you at all," Meredith offered.

And she was right, it wasn't. Normally, Annalise had an endless supply of patience and understanding with her staff.

She shook her head, agreeing with her friend.

"What happened downstairs to send you racing through the club like your ass was on fire?" Dominic asked. She hadn't even realized he was watching. "Did the guy you were with do something?"

"No." He hadn't done anything except assume she was interested in him because she'd given him her time and tried to make herself interested. "It wasn't his fault. The second he touched me…I had to get away."

God, she really hoped that she wouldn't go through the rest of her life with that kind of reaction anytime a man who wasn't Luca touched her. That would seriously suck. She enjoyed sex and physical intimacy way too much for that.

"You've been dealing with a lot. Robert's betrayal. And Luca's."

"He didn't betray me." Oh, it might have felt that way in the heat of the moment, but if she was honest with herself, he hadn't. He'd never promised her anything or lied to her. Sure, he'd ignored her wishes, but he'd been open about even that, uncaring that she didn't agree with him.

Dominic made a scoffing noise deep in his throat. "Maybe not technically, but he definitely left without a conversation, something you deserved. I saw the two of you down here that night. I know you were more than simply colleagues working on a project."

That was very true.

"Trust us when we say we understand how complicated it can get mixing business with pleasure." Meredith shot a knowing smile across at her fiancé.

"It wasn't like that between us. I knew from the start, based on what you'd told me about him, that Luca didn't do permanent. It isn't his fault that I turned stupid and fell in love with him."

The realization hit her like a bolt of lightning. She was in love with him. It was more than just him walking away without a word. If anyone else had done that, she wouldn't have cared. But Luca mattered. Until the words had come out of her mouth, Annalise wasn't even aware of just how much.

She hadn't let herself even think that possibility, because she knew it wouldn't do her any good. Luca was who he was. But clearly, there'd been a small place buried deep inside that had hoped he could be different with her.

And that was on her.

What she needed was time. That was all. If she could learn to live with the memories of her mother's death, she could learn to live with the reality of loving someone who didn't love her back.

"You could always go talk to him. I distinctly remember a late-night conversation where you told me to get my head out of my ass and fight for what I wanted."

Annalise was shaking her head before Meredith stopped speaking. "That was different. I knew Dominic was madly in love with you and just needed a shove."

Dominic's mouth twisted into a wry grin. "Gee, thanks."

She shrugged. "The truth hurts sometimes. But Luca isn't in love with me."

"How do you know that? From what I understand, Luca never exactly had an example of what love looks like. Maybe he just doesn't recognize what he feels."

For a brief second, hope snaked through her belly,

warm, seductive and oh so tempting. No, that wasn't going to help. She needed to be realistic right now.

"If he cared at all, he wouldn't have left the way he did. Or he would have come back by now. Just like all of his other projects, the problem was solved, and he walked away." Without a second glance. Surely, the pain of that would lessen over time.

"Look, I appreciate the support." And, really, wasn't that what she'd come to Excess looking for tonight? Not music, booze or unwanted company. She'd needed her brother and best friend. Their unwavering support.

"I feel a little better, actually. I'm going to head home, take tomorrow off and spend the day getting pampered at the spa. I haven't taken any time for myself in a very long while."

Meredith's hand curved around Annalise's shoulder and squeezed. "That sounds great. Do you want some company?"

Annalise thought about it for several moments, before saying, "Always. A girls' day is exactly what I need."

Fourteen

Luca stared at the bank of computer screens, hard drives and other electronic paraphernalia. He should be working. He should have been working for the past several days.

But he wasn't.

The problem he was supposed to be solving just couldn't hold his attention.

The peal of his front door alert saved him from pretending anymore.

Pushing up from his chair, Luca strode from the basement he'd set up as his workspace and through the house. The space echoed, making him realize just how empty it was. That fact had never bothered him before, but it did now. Annalise hadn't even been here that often, but the house missed her presence.

No, he missed her.

The last person Luca expected to see at his front door was Dominic Mercado. His first thought was that something had happened to Annalise. His heart stuttered deep inside his chest and everything flushed hot with dread. But then logic slipped in. Her brother had no reason to tell him even if something bad had happened.

No, this visit most likely had to do with Stone Surveillance and some project they wanted him involved with. He had been ignoring his phone for the last few days, so it was likely Stone had attempted to get in touch with him and when he couldn't, he'd sent the local backup.

Yanking the door open, Luca turned on his heel and trusted the other man would follow him into the kitchen. Considering his place was almost nine thousand square feet, surprisingly enough, he only used a fraction of it. If he was smart, he'd sell it. He'd bought the house a long time ago because when he'd started making money the one thing he'd wanted, something he'd never had before, was a home no one could take away from him.

And it made sense to buy the biggest and best he could afford. And he could afford a lot.

But what he'd failed to realize, until he'd seen Annalise in her own apartment, was that a house wasn't a home unless you had someone important to share it with.

Reaching into the fridge, Luca pulled out two bottles. Condensation slid down the cold glass as he popped the top and handed a beer to Dominic.

"To what do I owe the pleasure?" he finally asked.

Dominic didn't even bother to take a drink. He simply placed his bottle onto the island between them, pressed his palms to the granite and leaned forward. "Stop being an ass to my sister."

Luca rocked back on his heels. Okay, so this was about Annalise.

"I'm not being anything with your sister."

Dominic's dark eyebrows shot down into a harsh frown. "I'm fully aware. That's how you're being an ass."

Luca shook his head. "I don't understand."

"I saw the two of you, together in that hallway. Both of you are smart enough to realize cameras can be everywhere."

Luca didn't know whether to be shocked, amused or offended. "You watched your sister and I have sex?"

"God, no. I didn't have to. My head of security told me what was happening. He thought I'd want to know."

Luca fought the urge to roll his eyes. Even though Annalise was an adult and fully capable of making her own decisions, Dominic and his staff thought she'd needed babysitting.

"And did you?"

A grimace twisted Dominic's mouth. "Not particularly, but since I do know, I came here to do something I wish someone had done for me."

This should be interesting. Crossing his arms over his chest, Luca leaned back against the counter. "Which is?"

"Tell me to get my head out of my ass. Do you care about my sister?"

Luca didn't even hesitate to answer or contemplate lying. "Yes." The question was simple and the answer was even simpler.

"Then why did you walk away?"

"Because your sister will never trust me. She'll always see me as the cheater her father beat to hell and tossed out on the street. She told me to leave. That I wasn't wanted. I've been unwanted enough in my life and made myself a promise a long time ago not to overstay my welcome. I don't need anyone in my life who doesn't want me there. So, I did what she asked."

And it had hurt like hell.

More than being shuffled from place to place as a child. At some point in his life, he'd become immune to that initial hit when his caseworker would show up at the front door unannounced and tell him to pack his things. The real pain always came later, when he was alone in some strange new place with no one around who really gave a damn about him.

Once he'd reached adulthood, he'd promised himself that no one would ever have the power to hurt him that same way again. But apparently, he couldn't control that either...because Annalise had.

Dominic sank down onto one of the barstools pushed under the counter. The dark cloud that had swirled through his eyes slowly cleared.

Leaning toward Luca, Dominic gave him a long, studied look before saying, "She's a mess, man."

"I can imagine. I know she has to be taking Robert's betrayal like a punch to the gut."

Dominic shook his head. "Sure, that hurt. But not nearly as much as walking out of that room and finding you'd packed all your things and left without even a word. That devastated her."

"Bullshit." The word was out of his mouth before he even realized he intended to say it. "She told me to leave and knows where to find me. If she wanted to talk, to change her mind, she could have at any time."

Dominic's mouth twisted into a grimace. "Two more stubborn people I've never met."

Luca laughed, the sound coming out like gravel. "Something tells me you're the pot and I'm the kettle."

"She's in love with you, Luca. If you love her, you need to go talk to her."

Maybe he'd heard wrong. Luca stared across at Dominic, waiting for some clue as to what the other man had actually said. Because it couldn't be what he'd thought.

But when Dominic simply stared back, Luca realized his ears weren't malfunctioning. "No, she doesn't."

"Yes, she does. Trust me, I know my sister. Did you know? I can count on one hand the number of men Annalise has brought to my club since I opened it almost ten years ago."

Dominic slowly raised a single finger, and then tipped it to point at Luca's chest.

"Why do you think that is? It's not that she doesn't date, because she does. It's not that men haven't been involved in her life, because they have. But none of them were important enough to bring to my place for me to meet."

"You and I already knew each other."

"What does that have to do with anything?"

How could he not recognize the distinction? "That night wasn't about introducing me to her brother, Dominic. We'd already met and Annalise knew it. It was about letting off steam. It was about distraction."

"Bullshit. It was about bringing you to the place where she feels safe and seeing you interact with the two people who are most important in her life."

Something hot and hard bloomed through the center of Luca's chest. It was fragile and cut almost like glass. Hope hurt when every time he'd ever felt it, it had turned around to slice him open.

"I'm telling you, what happens next is up to you. Annalise knows you have a history of walking away, and in her mind that's exactly what you did, whether she told you to or not. You don't have long-term relationships. Hell, even with your work you simply solve a problem and then leave it for others to deal with the solution. I get why, but right now, you have a decision to make. Are you going to continue to let your past dictate your future? Or are you going to take a risk and reach for what you want?"

Luca shook his head. Hope and fear ground through his gut.

Dominic continued, "I'm here to tell you that life is messy and nothing is guaranteed, but fighting for love and happiness is always worth it."

Opening his mouth, Luca wasn't even sure what he would have said, but Dominic's raised hand stopped him. "You don't have to say anything. In fact, I'd rather you didn't. This is between you and my sister. I'm just here as a friend telling you that I think there are things you both need to talk about before you turn your back on the possibility of something important."

Without waiting for a response, Dominic pushed up from the stool and left.

Luca stood there, in the kitchen, his beer going flat and warm in the bottle. He stared across the room and listened to the silence.

The last few days had sucked. Not because he couldn't concentrate, or because his work wasn't co-operating. But because Annalise hadn't been in them.

Dominic was right. Luca had spent his entire life being disappointed, but Annalise hadn't once let him down. She'd fought with him. Disagreed with him. Laughed with him and shared pieces of her soul with him.

He owed it to them both to at least see if there was a possibility for more.

Meredith had shown up at Annalise's apartment around ten. They'd spent the morning in the spa getting facials, massages and salt scrubs. Every inch of her skin tingled.

She should have felt relaxed and rejuvenated, but she didn't.

Annalise had forced herself to go through the motions. She pretended to be happy—or at least happier than she'd been last night. She wasn't sure Meredith was buying the act, but she was firmly living "fake it till you make it" today.

They'd had trays of food—finger sandwiches, chicken salad, pasta salad, fruit and veggies—catered into the spa for lunch. Now they were both getting mani-pedis and debating the choice between siren red and seashell pink.

Meredith wanted Annalise to go with red, but right now she just wasn't feeling the bold, vibrant color. At the moment, she was more muted and pastel.

"Don't listen to her. The red." Meredith yanked the bottle of pink away and stuffed it behind her back.

"Very mature, Meredith. Give me the bottle."

She shook her head. "Not on your life. Trust me. What you need is something fun."

What Annalise needed was a nap—she hadn't slept well for days—and a couple of aspirin for the headache that had been on the edge of her brain all day.

A commotion at the front of the spa stopped any protest she might have made.

"Sir, you can't go back there."

A low growl was apparently the only response.

Great, just what she needed. A crisis to deal with. She might not run the spa, but she managed the entire casino, which meant a problem occurring in her presence required her attention. And if some asshole was pushing his way through the women to harass a customer, that was something she needed to address.

Hopping up out of the chair, Annalise hobbled over with her half-painted toes and collided with a hard wall of muscle as she exited into the hallway.

"Ooomph." The sound rushed out of her, along with every speck of oxygen in her lungs.

Hard hands gripped her upper arms, holding her steady even as she rocked back onto her heels. Looking down, Annalise realized bright red polish had smeared all over the black Italian leather of an expensive pair of loafers.

Well, hell.

Her body buzzed and her mind spun. Her stomach flipped sideways and then upside down, somersaulting through her.

Instinct told her who held her, long before her

gaze moved up the long, muscled frame of his body to stare into those stormy gray eyes.

"What are you doing here?" she whispered, the words somehow sticking in her throat.

"Your brother came to see me."

Annalise was going to kill him.

Her mouth contorted into a grimace. Slowly, she disengaged from his hold. "I'm sorry." Luca wasn't there because he'd realized he couldn't live without her. He was there because Dominic had played the big brother card and probably threatened him.

The hope that had taken flight in her chest crashed into a leaden weight through the pit of her belly.

Twisting, she glared at Meredith, who was sitting silently behind them, shamelessly drinking in every moment. "Did you know Dominic was going to do this?"

Meredith shrugged, completely unrepentant and unapologetic about her fiancé's behavior.

Annalise would deal with her meddling brother and betraying best friend later.

Snatching Luca's arm, she pushed him out into the hallway and pointedly shut the door behind them.

The hallway was quiet. She could hear the soft, elegant tinkle of bells and relaxation music coming from a door farther down. They were surrounded by dark wood and pale floors. Tranquility that was designed to de-stress.

Right at this moment, Annalise felt far from tranquil.

Luca opened his mouth, but she shook her head. They weren't going to do this in the hallway. Heading to the end, she opened a door and pushed him inside.

A long padded table sat in the middle of the room. Soft, glowing light shone from a lamp in the corner of the space. Great, just what she needed—mood lighting.

Purposely rounding the table, she placed it between them. "I apologize for whatever Dominic said. He was out of line and I'll have a talk with him."

Luca ignored the clear signals she was giving and deliberately scooted around the foot of the table to follow her. Suddenly, the room that normally seemed intimate and relaxing became very, very small. All the oxygen disappeared, and Annalise had a difficult time pulling in a single breath.

She should move. But she didn't. Instead, she stood there, feet cemented to the floor, as Luca wrapped his hands around her upper arms again.

He tugged, gently, urging her forward.

And like an idiot, she went. Nothing good could come from this except more pain. But apparently, she was a glutton for punishment.

Slowly, his palm slipped beneath the heavy fall of her hair. Cupping the nape of her neck, Luca pulled her up onto her toes until his mouth found hers.

The kiss was…everything. Heat swirled through her belly, settling at the apex of her thighs in a throbbing rush. But beneath the physical reaction, there was more.

The taste of grief and hope, sharp and tangy on his tongue. A lump formed in the back of Annalise's throat. Slowly, he teased her with his lips until she finally opened for him. A rush of relief accompanied the stroke of his tongue into her mouth.

Tears stung the backs of her eyes.

No. Annalise shoved him away.

"No, I'm not going to do this, Luca. I can't. It hurts too much. I know it isn't your fault and I'm not asking for anything, except that you leave me alone. Loving you, knowing that you'll never love me… It's too much. I can't just wait and quietly take whatever crumbs you feel like giving me whenever you want to. I need more. I deserve mor—"

Her words broke off as his fingers touched her lips to quiet her. His breath was ragged, his eyes burned into her soul, but his mouth tipped up in a tentative smile.

"You're right. You deserve more. I love you, Annalise. It scares the shit out of me. No one in my entire life has ever chosen me. My parents died and no one stepped up to take me. No family, no friends. No foster family fought to keep me. I watched as other kids in the system were adopted, but never me. Sometimes I don't believe I deserve to be loved or wanted."

God, that broke her heart because he did deserve to be loved.

Reaching up, she cupped his face with the palm of her hand. No matter what else happened between them, if she could make him believe that, then everything would be worth it.

"You're an amazing man, Luca, and I have no doubt you were equally amazing as a child. All those people, your foster families, missed out. Not having you in their lives is their loss, and no reflection on your worth. You are worthy of love. I love you."

Luca swallowed, the long column of his throat working hard.

"When you told me to leave, that I wasn't wanted…that was my worst fear come to life."

God, he was killing her. "I'm sorry, Luca. I didn't think about what I was saying or how those words might make you feel. I knew that the job was over, the puzzle solved, and that history said you'd leave. I was protecting myself, even though I didn't realize it. Knowing you were going to leave on top of Robert's betrayal…"

Luca's hand squeezed her shoulder. "*Your* worst nightmare come to life."

Annalise swallowed hard as she nodded.

In trying to protect themselves, they'd both managed to hurt each other. Annalise gazed up at Luca and realized that knowing she'd hurt Luca in that way was much worse than any pain she might feel herself.

"I promise to never walk away again. I want you in my life, Annalise. You're worth taking a risk for, worth sticking around for."

A smile lit her eyes, the heat of happiness blazing through her chest. "I'll always choose you."

A groan slipping through his parted lips, Luca lifted her into the air and dropped her onto the padded table. His mouth found hers and his hands started tugging off her clothes.

"Luca," she protested. "We can't."

Pulling back, a wicked twinkle in his steel eyes, he said, "You're the boss, Annalise. You can do whatever you want to."

And darn if he wasn't right.

Epilogue

Joker stared down at the glowing bank of screens in front of him. All around him, inky night pressed in. The blinking cursor taunted him, tempting him with the consequences of what he was about to do. Should he? Shouldn't he?

Oh, he knew the answer, but…

The loud trill of a song about being too sexy made him jump. Cursing, Joker jerked his accusing gaze to the cell phone sitting on the charging stand beside him.

How the hell did he *know*?

Joker should have changed the song a long time ago but had to admit a little pride that his friend had managed to break into his phone and change the ringtone for his calls.

Gray Lockwood's name scrolled across the screen, although clearly, Joker didn't need the visual clue to know who was calling. He and Gray had a history. Mutual friends had introduced them while Gray was in prison serving time for embezzling money from the family business. A charge he was innocent of, although only a handful of people knew the truth.

Joker had helped him identify the person who had framed him. Little did they know that person would turn out to be a half sister Gray had never known existed.

Guilt slipped through Joker's chest, although he had no idea why. There was no possible way Gray could know what he was contemplating.

His friend would find it suspicious if he didn't answer, though, so Joker picked up the phone and hit the big green button.

"Hey, man. What's up?"

"I just thought you'd want to know everything went down at the Magnifique tonight. They caught the man responsible for the theft and he's currently being booked."

It was nice that Gray had called, although Joker was already aware. Information was the key to knowledge and knowledge was the key that unlocked everything important in life. But it wasn't worth explaining that. So, instead, he simply said, "Great. I'm glad things worked out."

They usually did whenever he was involved, not that he was cocky or anything. Just realistic and honest. He was that good at what he did, which wasn't surprising since he'd been hacking since he was fourteen. Which was why Gray and Stone Surveillance, the investigative firm he partially owned, kept Joker on retainer.

A beep from one of his screens pulled Joker's attention. Goddammit, she was moving money already. He really needed to get off this phone and make a decision before she slipped away again. It was dumb luck that he'd found her this time.

"Was there something else?" he asked, distracted.

The long pause from the other end of the line finally caught his attention.

Gray slowly asked, "How is she?"

Joker grimaced. Of course Gray would be asking that right now. "You told me not to tell you."

A heavy sigh echoed through the phone. "I was being an idiot when I said that. Jameson, I need to know. It's been almost a year and the last time I saw her someone was shooting at her. Just…is she okay?"

Joker really disliked his given name, but it meant something that Gray had used it, because he never did. He heard the desperation in the man's voice and really hated it.

Because he felt it too.

"She's good."

For the moment. Kinley Sullivan was fine right

now, but if she kept going, there was no doubt she'd end up dead.

Gray's little sister—half sister—currently spent her life operating as a modern-day Robin Hood, stealing money from criminals and redistributing the wealth to those who needed it.

Bad people were after her. Joker had been watching her trail for months, both impressed with her hacking skills and pissed that she was taking the kind of risks that would one day put her life in jeopardy. And frustrated because there was nothing he could do to stop her.

She'd done something very stupid. Stealing money from the wrong man, someone who was as ruthless as he was relentless. Joker wasn't the only person looking for Kinley...and he also wasn't the only one who'd finally found her.

"Thanks, man," Gray said, not pushing for more details. Which was good, because Joker really didn't want to give them to him.

He was relieved when his friend finally hung up.

And he could return his attention to the screen and the blinking cursor. Once he hit the button to run the program, there was no going back.

A knot of dread dropped into his belly, but Joker didn't see any other way. Kinley had been avoiding him for months, just one step ahead and out of his grasp.

But now, with someone else breathing down her neck, she needed to come in. Gray and Stone Sur-

veillance would protect her, even if she didn't believe her brother would have her back because she'd
once betrayed him.

Wiping out her accounts would leave her with no
resources and make her even more of a sitting duck.

But it was the only way he knew to force her hand.

Force her to come to him for help.

Hitting the button, the program ran and on the
screen the numbers ticked down from billions to
zero.

* * * * *

*Read Joker's story, coming soon,
only from Harlequin Desire!*

*And don't miss a single story in the
Bad Billionaires series*

The Rebel's Redemption
The Devil's Bargain
The Sinner's Secret
Secrets, Vegas Style

COMING NEXT MONTH FROM

HARLEQUIN
DESIRE

#2893 VACATION CRUSH
Texas Cattleman's Club: Ranchers and Rivals
by Yahrah St. John
What do you do after confessing a crush on an accidental livestream? Take a vacation to escape the gossip! But when Natalie Hastings gets to the resort, her crush—handsome rancher Jonathan Lattimore—is there too. Will one little vacation fling be enough?

#2894 THE MARRIAGE MANDATE
Dynasties: Tech Tycoons • by Shannon McKenna
Pressured into marrying, heiress Maddie Moss chooses the last man in the world her family will accept—her brother's ex–business partner, Jack Daly. Accused of destroying the company, Jack can use the opportunity to finally prove his innocence—but only if he can resist Maddie...

#2895 A RANCHER'S REWARD
Heirs of Hardwell Ranch • by J. Margot Critch
To earn a large inheritance, playboy rancher Garrett Hardwell needs a fake fiancée—fast! Wedding planner Willa Statler is the best choice. The problem? She's his best friend's younger sister! With so much at stake, will their very real connection ruin everything?

#2896 SECOND CHANCE VOWS
Angel's Share • by Jules Bennett
Despite their undeniable chemistry, Camden Preston and Delilah Hawthorn are separating. With divorce looming, Delilah is shocked when her blind date at a masquerade gala turns out to be her husband! The attraction's still there, but can they overcome what tore them apart?

#2897 BLACK SHEEP BARGAIN
Billionaires of Boston • by Naima Simone
Abandoned at birth, CEO Nico Morgan will upend the one thing his father loved most—his company. Integral to the plan is a charming partner, and that's his ex, Athena Evans. But old feelings and hot passion could derail everything...

#2898 SECRET LIVED AFTER HOURS
The Kane Heirs • by Cynthia St. Aubin
Finding his father's assistant at an underground fight club, playboy Mason Kane realizes he isn't the only one leading a double life. So he offers Charlotte Westbrook a whirlwind Riviera fling to help her loosen up, but it could cost her job and her heart...

YOU CAN FIND MORE INFORMATION ON UPCOMING HARLEQUIN TITLES, FREE EXCERPTS AND MORE AT HARLEQUIN.COM.

HDCNM0722

*Home due to tragedy, exes Felicity Vance and
Wynn Oliver don't expect to see one another, but Wynn
needs a caregiver for the baby niece now entrusted in
his care. But when one hot night changes everything,
will secrets from their past ruin it all?*

Read on for a sneak peek at
The Comeback Heir
by USA TODAY *bestselling author Janice Maynard*

"This won't work. You know it won't." Felicity
continued. "If the baby is your priority, then you and
I can't..."

Can't what?" Wynn smiled mockingly.

"You're taunting me, but I don't know why."

"You don't want to *enjoy* each other while you're
here?"

"We had our chance. We didn't make it work. And
I'm not one for fooling around just for a few orgasms."

"The old Fliss never said things like that."

"The old *Felicity* was an eighteen-year-old kid."

"You always seemed mature for your age. You had
a vision for your future and you made it happen. I'm
proud of you."

She gaped at him. "Thank you."

"I'm sorry," he said gruffly. "I shouldn't have kissed you. Let's pretend it never happened. A fresh start, Fliss. Please?"

"Of course. We're both here to honor Shandy and care for her daughter. I don't think we should do anything to mess that up."

"Agreed."

Don't miss what happens next in...
The Comeback Heir
by USA TODAY *bestselling author Janice Maynard.*

Available September 2022 wherever
Harlequin Desire books and ebooks are sold.

Harlequin.com

HDEXP0722R